THE PUMPKINHEAD ADVENTURES:
PILGRIM'S SECRET

THE PUMPKINHEAD ADVENTURES: PILGRIM'S SECRET

WAYNE & CAROLYN CARTER-MARCINKIEWICZ

Thank God, Lord Jesus Christ and the Holy Spirit

To my wife Carolyn Carter-Marcinkiewicz

To my parents Mom and Dad

The owners of the furniture factories
and all of the employees, Mom and Dad

The best comedians ever to grace the planet in my opinion,

Moe, Larry, Curly, Shemp, Abbott and Costello

CHAPTER ONE

THE FARMHOUSE

It was a very humid Memorial Day in the small town of Gardner, Massachusetts. Brothers Wayne and Matt visited friends in an effort to embark upon an adventure to explore an abandoned farmhouse. They packed their cars with supplies and drove to Shady Pines Cemetery. Both brothers were teenagers and drove Wayne's 1970 Chevelle SS. Their friends Mark and Sam were outside washing Sam's 1969 GTO. "We better leave before it becomes dark," said Wayne. It was much later than they thought when they loaded all of the supplies they needed in the trunks of their cars.

It was dark and the fog engulfed the town making the full moon barely visible. Several dirt roads converged at the center of the cemetery. The woods surrounded the entire-area and the main entrance was accessible from Townsend Road. With great trepidation, they entered the graveyard. Two sets of headlights pierced through the fog. As they approached the main entrance, the full moon disappeared behind a few clouds. Both cars slowly came to a screeching halt. The noise of the collective engines was deafening.

Wayne scanned the area and noticed two of the ugliest gargoyles resting upon the pillars. "What are we doing here?" asked Matt. Wayne opened the window replying, "I thought that we would check out the farmhouse in the woods." They slowly entered the graveyard. The moon appeared brighter as they drove deeper into the wooded area. They drove down a slight ravine to the back of the cemetery. A narrow road led further into the woods towards a small clearing. As they exited the vehicles, Matt glanced at the night sky where the moon illuminated the trees casting enough light for them to explore.

They took their backpacks out of the cars and found a new spot to relax and sip root beer. "Let's check out the old farmhouse which has been our goal for several years," said Matt. They began to slowly walk, shining their flashlights and stumbled upon a river about ten feet wide. A few yards to the right was an old broken- down bridge. They looked at one another, "Well who is going to go first?" "The right side of the bridge appears to be safer," said Matt. "I'll go first," said Wayne. He started to walk across the bridge on the right and could feel and hear the wood cracking beneath. "Take it very slowly dude," said Sam. Wayne reached the other side of the river. They began to take turns crossing it. Sam was the last to cross and about the halfway mark his left leg went through it. He screamed and proceeded to pull his leg out of the hole. He finally made it to the other side. "Don't be scared guys," said Matt. They looked up at the sky and saw a falling star. "I think it means good luck when you see a falling star," said Sam.

Matt tripped and fell over a small rock. "Hey guy, are you alright?" asked Wayne. "Yeah, I think so. I scraped my knee, but I'll be alright," said Matt. They walked another one hundred feet into the woods. When they saw the enormous barn, it stopped them in their tracks. The barn was about two hundred feet long and about seventy feet wide. There were a dozen holes throughout the roof and the cupola was caving in the center. It was completely deteriorated.

They stood in the front of the entrance to the barn wondering what course of action should be taken. A pungent musty aroma emanated from the inside. "Who is going to enter first?" asked Matt. "Well, I will and you three had better follow me!" said Wayne. He slowly walked into the barn, noticing horse stalls on both sides. The doors were missing and the stalls housed some chicken wire. There were carcasses of animals. They scanned the hay loft and Wayne retrieved a ladder. It appeared to be unsafe, but he slowly ascended the ladder. He treaded carefully until he landed in the loft. "I made it! I'll look around up here. You guys keep looking down there," said Wayne.

He slowly canvassed the area, taking his time and noticed there was very little hay and a couple of decaying pitchforks dangling from the nails in the wall along with an antique rusted pulley system for hauling the hay up to the loft. "There isn't much going on here," said Wayne. He took a step in the middle of the hay loft and heard a loud crack beneath his feet. He descended through the floor. He quickly held onto one of the rafters beneath the floor. "Guys I need your help!" he said. They looked at one another and said: "Hold on, we are coming to the rescue!" They ran underneath him and asked what he wanted them to do to which he replied, "Get something to break my fall!" They gathered a few bales of hay and piled them below his feet. "Whenever you are ready, you can drop," said Matt. Wayne couldn't wait any longer and fell, landing in a pile of hay. He stood up cracking his neck from left to right. "Are you alright?" said Sam. "I'll live thank God," said Wayne.

CHAPTER TWO

NATIVE AMERICAN SETTLERS

The boys realized that the barn had been empty for a long time. The general consensus was to explore the farmhouse. They immediately exited the barn illuminating the wooded path with their flashlights. "I hope that we don't run into Sasquatch," said Wayne. They laughed but became somber when the howling of a coyote was heard in the distance. They became frightened and decided to leave the woods. As they were running, they noticed the house and ran to the front entrance. Their collective curiosity was piqued and they ran to the door to the abandoned house. Matt decided to go first and literally ripped the door off of its hinge, slamming it on the ground.

As they slowly entered the house, swiping off cobwebs, they realized that it had been abandoned for several years. '"Hello is anyone here?" asked Wayne. They walked down the hallway entering what used to be the kitchen. There wasn't much left but a rusty wood stove and a counter which was deteriorating. The floorboards appeared to be intact. "Be careful where you walk," said Sam. "I think that I have seen enough in this room," said Matt. Wayne looked around the corner to see if it was safe to enter. They continued to explore finding an empty chest. "I've seen enough," said Matt.

They began walking when Wayne accidentally flashed his light to the right corner of the room. It uncovered something shiny emitting through the floor. "Hey guys, I think I see something," said Wayne. Wayne went over to the corner and began to rip up the boards. "Well done!" said Matt. To say that they were stunned was a gross understatement. They stared at the trap door in disbelief. Wayne seized the handle of the trap door lifting it and leaning it against the wall. He exposed what appeared to be a primitive tunnel going into the ground. They shined the flashlights into the tunnel, but they couldn't see anything until they glimpsed a wooden ladder that descended into the hole. "This is very interesting and calls for a cola. I need all of the caffeine I can consume at this point," said Wayne.

They decided that Wayne would be the first to descend the ladder into the tunnel. Matt asked: "Do you see anything yet?" "I think that I am near the bottom," said Wayne. He felt the ground beneath his feet. "Leave one person up there just in case something goes wrong," said Wayne. Matt and Sam glanced at one another. They descended the ladder single file to view a hidden bunker. It was approximately twenty by thirty feet. Their lights illuminated partial remains of another voyager. "Do you think that we should go?" asked Matt. "We've come this far and should continue to look around a little longer," said Wayne.

They began searching and located an old chest. "I haven't found anything yet," said Matt. "Hey, did you look at this?" asked Mark. "It looks like a chain in the wall, but I'm uncertain as to what it is doing here," said Matt. "Do you think they were attempting to protect something? Because we haven't found anything yet," said Mark. They began to focus on the chain. "Give it a pull," said Wayne. They tugged the chain and pulled it with all of their might opening a small concrete door halfway from the wall. They looked at one another not believing their eyes. They were coughing due to the stale air coming out of the chamber.

Wayne glanced at the remains of the voyagers and playfully said, "We've got it guys, you don't need to help us." "Hey did you find anything down there?" asked Sam. "Silence!" said Wayne. "Who is going to go first this time?" asked Wayne. "I'll go first," said Matt. They followed Matt on their hands and knees since the entrance was too small for anyone to stand upright. They finally were able to stand in a small room which was approximately five by twelve feet. They looked around the room and noticed a large amount of dirt. "Well, just a pile of dirt," said Matt.

They walked towards the dirt when Wayne kicked something

shiny. "Hey what is that which you kicked up from the dirt?" asked Mark. Wayne bent down and retrieved what appeared to be a coin. He brushed the dirt off the coin. "You know what this means, we are millionaires," said Matt. Wayne and Mark laughed. "Not with one coin, we're not," said Wayne. "Well, there is more where that came from," said Matt.

"I think that whatever was here in the past was gone centuries ago," said Wayne. "Do you think that the gold came over with the pilgrims?" asked Matt. "It could be possible. In the past, gold was well hidden and it is possible that it was a secret only known to a few people," said Wayne. He placed the gold coin back in his pocket.

"I think that we should attempt to dig in the dirt pile," said Wayne. They began digging with their hands. Approximately twenty minutes into it, they decided to quit. Wayne wanted to devote a few more minutes to search. Ten more minutes passed and then Matt screamed, "You were right!" They exposed a large chest. They stepped away from it for a few seconds in shock that this could really be the treasure. "Is it a treasure chest?" asked Matt. "It is turning out to be a great night," said Matt.

They stood in front of the chest. When they lifted the top of it, they noticed it was locked. "Now what do we do?" asked Matt. "Let me think," said Wayne. "Maybe our buddies in the next room have the keys," said Wayne. Matt exited the chamber and stood over the remains of the deceased pilgrims. He slipped his hands into the back pockets of their uniforms when he heard something move. It turned out to be the key to open the chest.

CHAPTER THREE

WHAT IS THE NAME OF THIS LOCATION?

Sam paced back and forth, waiting for his friends to return form the bunker. He walked over to what used to be a window. Looking into the night he noticed a full moon illuminating the sky. He gazed out at the pine trees scattered throughout the forest. Hundreds of years ago it was probably a rural farmland. Sam spoke to himself aloud saying, "The guys better hurry up, it is a little cumbersome being here all alone. I would have stayed home if I knew I was going to be the lookout!"

Sam began doing his karate moves to pass the time, speaking to himself, "I don't think so pal, just keep on moving before you get hurt." He was a little afraid of his own shadow when the moonlight danced through the window. Facing the window once more, he thought he saw a shadow moving from tree to tree, but resolved it to be an overactive imagination. Closing his eyes for a few seconds, "My eyes are playing tricks on me. There is nothing out there. I know no one else followed us here. We didn't tell anyone what we were doing. Well at least I know I didn't tell anyone. Maybe big foot does exist." He crawled over to the bunker trying to keep out of sight. He yelled, "Stop playing around you guys. I know that you are trying to scare me, but it won't work." There wasn't any answer, so he thought of going to the bunker in case they were in trouble.

He crawled back over to the window to see if it was the guys. He slightly peeked over the window sill and didn't see anything moving.

He breathed a sigh of relief. Perhaps, it was just another shadow of a tree. He thought it was ridiculous and tried to remain calm.

He thought he noticed a figure with a bow and arrow in his hands. An arrow passed very close to his head and he screamed. He awakened from a deep sleep and found himself in the abandoned house looking down at the bunker. There was still no sign of the others. He knew the only choice was to wait patiently.

CHAPTER FOUR

THE FIND

Click! That was the right key, now is the moment of truth," said Wayne. They lifted the lid of the chest and said in unison "We're rich!" Finally, the chest was opened and they looked inside. Their jaws dropped, "Is this some kind of joke? The chest is empty," said the boys. There was nothing left except an old bag. Wayne seized the old satchel from the chest. It was wrapped not unlike an old scroll. Slowly unrolling it revealed several old papers and a key which dropped out from the tightly wrapped papers. With astonishment, they wondered if they could sell it to a museum. "I don't think that we will be giving this to anyone," said Wayne.

Perusing through each individual sheet, they studied the map. "Perhaps we have found an answer," said Wayne. "They all have an X mark not unlike a treasure map. We have to figure out the true meaning of the markings. Let's roll them back up and I will pocket the key. "Let's get out of here," said Wayne. They exited the small bunker and called to Sam, "Relax, we are all done here," said Wayne. Wayne began climbing the rungs of the ladder. About halfway one of the rungs collapsed sending Wayne plummeting twenty feet onto the others. "Hey thanks guys," said Wayne. "Relax guys, Sam send a rope down," said Wayne. "I can't pull you guys up. You are too heavy," said Sam. "Tie it to one of the trees outside the house," said Matt. Sam quickly retrieved the rope from his backpack and went outside. He noticed what appeared to be several old graves with crosses marking the remaining ones.

Sam ran to the closest tree and tied a rope around it. He tossed it in the window and down to the bunker. Wayne came out of the bunker first and then the others followed suit. "What did you find down there?" asked Sam. They looked at one another and answered that they had not found much, except the satchel and several old papers. Wayne told them that he wanted to locate the marks on the maps while on summer vacation. "Let's get out of here and study the maps at the house," said Wayne.

They exited the room into the hallway. Sam was the last one to exit and noticed something shiny on the floor, He followed it to the hallway. It was the glimmer of an arrow lying dormant on the floor. "Let's get out of here guys," he said. They went into their cars and quickly exited the area checking the rear-view mirror. "I'm glad that we are out of the cemetery," said Sam. With a collective sigh of relief, they drove far away.

CHAPTER FIVE

THE QUEST

Pensively they sat outside on the stone wall which separated Wayne's parents' home and the cemetery. "Well, we have looked at these maps one hundred times. They don't give us too much information as to where the treasure might be," said Wayne. "'We know this one shows a hill or maybe a mountain and halfway down it is marked with the letter X," said Matt. "The closest mountain is Wachusett Mountain," said Sam. "We can give it a try and check it out," said Wayne. "l don't think that we should because something bad might happen," said Matt. "What could happen Matt? It's not easy cutting plywood in the dark. Let's go and look and if we don't find anything, then the map was a hoax," said Wayne. "Well who is with me?" said Wayne. All of the boys put their hands together in agreement.

They came prepared with every contingency in place in case the adventure became dangerous. They headed down the road in their cars passing through a few New England towns before embarking upon the rough terrain of the mountain. "It doesn't get better than this," said Sam. There was a silence in the car. Matt looked at Sam wondering if he was alright. He reassured Sam that if there were any signs of danger that they would immediately return home.

They reached the top of the mountain and slowly descended down the other side. Approximately one quarter mile Wayne pulled into a rocky road that ended a few hundred feet from the main road. They exited their vehicles. "Is this the place?" asked Matt. "There is no other place around, so this must be it," said

Wayne. "Well on the map it should be one hundred feet in that direction," said Matt.

Pointing up the hill they noticed a house to the left. It was condemned. "Hey guys, isn't that the house everyone says is haunted?" asked Matt. "We are not entering the house this time Matt. We are only interested in what lies ahead of us. We had better get a move on before it becomes dark," said Sam.

They carefully ascended the mountain. They began trudging through the brush, breaking small branches on the way. "We've gone more than one hundred feet, maybe two hundred feet," said Matt. "Let's split up in all four directions and begin looking for something out of the ordinary," said Wayne.

Each one went in a different direction. Matt went to the right, fighting through prickly bushes. "This is just great, getting cut up and for what nothing that's what," said Sam. He continued despite numerous obstacles. "We are just getting nowhere fast!" said Sam. "Nothing here guys. Let's just go home," said Sam. Sam came out of the bushes into a small clearing. That is when he looked up the hill and saw a large cliff overhanging what looked like it might have been someone's home hundreds of years ago built right into the rocks.

CHAPTER SIX

ANCIENT RUINS

Sam called to the guys, "Hey I think I've found something over here!" "Do you think that this is what we have been looking for? None of us found anything, so maybe this is the X on the map," said Sam. "You found it little man, right on," said Wayne. They ascended several steps that led into numerous rooms in the rock. "It must have taken years to blast through all of the rock to make one dozen rooms," said Wayne. The rooms varied in size. There were narrow passage ways connecting all of the rooms. They lowered their heads each time they entered a room. "They were short people," said Matt. "Let's just search and see if we can find a secret passage," said Sam. "We must be missing something," said Wayne. "Most of the rooms are empty except for a few old blankets and animal carcasses," said Sam. "Well we weren't the only ones that found this place," said Wayne. "Let's continue searching until we find something, o.k. guys," said Wayne.

"This is becoming ridiculous looking for a treasure that is probably not even here," said Matt. "It can't be more ridiculous than a car coming to life," said Wayne. "You have a point there," said Matt. They continued diligently searching each room until Wayne came upon a stone cross extending from a wall in one of the rooms. "Hey guys, I think I have found something," said Wayne. They crammed themselves into the tiny room to view the cross which extended out of the wall. Wayne explained that everyone during those times possessed a cross. He dusted it off and it revealed several emeralds throughout its structure. "Wow! Maybe that is the treasure of the map," said

Matt. "Why not show a cross on the map instead of an X?" asked Sam. "Good question," said Wayne.

Wayne began pulling on it attempting to break it free. "This cross is not budging," said Wayne. "Give me a hand Matt," said Wayne. "On the count of three we will pull it. Do you see what I see? It appears to be a door to something behind it," said Wayne. They glanced at the opening of the cross. They shined the flashlight through its narrow opening. It revealed stairs of stone leading upward into complete darkness. "It looks like a never-ending staircase," said Sam. "Well we might as well head up the stairs, and I'll lead the way as usual," said Wayne.

They began to ascend the stairs, clearing the cobwebs as they went and touching the wall on both sides. "Are we there yet?" asked Sam. "Keep the peanut gallery to a minimum. Thank you," said Wayne. They were engulfed in darkness until they shined the light ahead of them illuminating the stairway.

Spiders and other insects were crawling on the walls. They began swatting all of the cobwebs as they climbed the stairs. They began to cough as the air became stale. "We must be reaching the summit," said Matt. They finally came to an abrupt end facing a wall.

"What is this, a stairway to nowhere?" asked Matt. "It looks that way," said Sam. "Hey guys, what is that handle above your head?" asked Matt. "Well, just pull on it," said Sam. "You think that the wall is just going to open up?" asked Wayne. "Well yeah, it did at the bottom of the stairs," said Matt. "Well you have a point there," said Wayne. "Just pull on it so we can get out of here," said Matt. "Do it!" they cried in unison.

Wayne pulled as hard as he could on the old rusty handle. It began to budge very slowly. "That's it guy, you have it," said Matt. The handle started to extend more from the wall when it came out completely. "Now you did it, you broke it man," said Matt. "I told you that it was rusted. Let's just turn our back and get out of here," said Wayne.

Suddenly they heard a rumbling sound behind the wall. "Who knows we might get out of here quicker than we think," said Matt. "Let's go because nothing is happening here," said Sam. The rumbling became louder and as soon as they turned around to descend the stairs the platform disintegrated underneath. One by one they went down the slide made out of stone. Wayne put out his hands to try to slow down, but couldn't get a grip on the cold stone. "Hang on I think we are done for now. I think that we are going in the wrong direction if we are going to meet our maker," said Wayne.

CHAPTER SEVEN

ACROBATIC SKILLS

They quickly shot out of a large hole into a chamber, landing on their behinds. "That was a very painful landing. What did we land on anyway?" "I don't know, but I have something very painful digging in my back," said Matt. He seized the object behind his back and pulled it out with his hands. "Give me some light over here guys," said Matt. Wayne hit the side of the flashlight to get it to work. He illuminated the area over where he thought they might be. They all looked at what Matt had in his hands. "Guys, this looks like a human skull," said Sam. Matt dropped the skull. They all stood up and looked around and noticed some unlit torches embedded within the wall. Wayne went over to light each one.

"Where did we end up? This is someone's idea of a sick joke, that is what it is," said Wayne. "How are we getting out of this mess?" asked Matt. "Well let's look around and find a way out before we end up like these guys. There must be some secret passage somewhere," said Wayne. "I think we found more of the settlers. Perhaps, we can find our next clue to the treasure," said Sam. "How about you and your brother look for a way out and Matt and I will look for clues," said Wayne.

Wayne and Matt split up looking for clues. They searched for hours looking for any small clue to the treasure. Wayne came upon another deceased settler leaning against the wall clenching something in his hand. Wayne slowly opened his hand and a few gold coins fell from it. "Hey, I found a few more gold coins," he said.

Matt and Sam went over to look at the gold coins in his hands. "Now we are finally getting somewhere," said Matt. Sam looked at the deceased pilgrim when he noticed a leather satchel behind him. "Look guys, a leather satchel," he said. "Open it up and see what is really inside," said Matt. Sam removed an animal hide and Matt turned it over. It appeared to be another map. They all stared at it for several minutes.

The map showed a very large pine tree in the middle. In front it was a small mark that looked like an X. "This is going to be hard to find," said Wayne. "This was made so long ago. What about the other maps we found?" asked Matt. "Let's just concentrate on this for now," said Wayne. "That is really good guys, but we have one problem. We haven't even found a way out yet," said Sam. "The bad news is I don't think there is a way out," said Sam. "Yeah, just look around us. There are several deceased settlers here. I'm sure if they had found a way out, they would have survived," said Matt.

"Well Sam, you have been looking for a way out, have you found anything?" asked Wayne. "The only thing I did find was over here is where someone was digging," said Sam. The boys gathered around Sam. "This is the only wall that doesn't feel like rock," said Sam. They began to dig into the dirt, mud and small stones. "We need something with more leverage," said Wayne. They seized a few boards that were on the ground. They dug for several hours and still came up with nothing. They were sweating and breathing heavily. "Hey guys, I think I broke a nail," laughed Sam. "Yeah, you would break a nail," laughed Wayne. They all began to laugh out loud.

They noticed it was very hard to breathe and it became repressive as a sauna. "I think the only oxygen we are getting is from the area we slid out of," said Matt. Then they looked at one another. "Just maybe we can reach the hole with our acrobatic skills," laughed Wayne. "Even if we reach the hole, there is no way of getting up to that side.

CHAPTER EIGHT

THE ESCAPE

They heard a faint voice. It almost sounded like a little girl. They recognized the voice. It was Sam who was still digging. "Hey guys, I think I see what looks like daylight through the small hole I made," said Sam. "I felt a rush of fresh air," said Sam. They ran to see what Sam was talking about. They looked through the small hole one at a time. "I think Sam saved us. It looks like a blue sky," said Matt.

"Let's see if you are right Matt," said Wayne. Wayne pushed Sam against the wall and when it collapsed Sam flew down a small embankment. They began to laugh except for Sam. "Guys, that really wasn't funny, now that I have mud all over me," said Sam. The rest of the boys stepped out onto the mud and debris into the fresh air. "You were right Sam. We are still alive because of your great determination,' said Wayne. "Thanks," said Sam as he slowly brushed the mud of his clothes.

The boys met Sam down the embankment. They looked back to where they had just exited. "I think that we were very lucky," said Wayne. "Why is that, may I ask?" said Matt. "I say with all of the erosion which occurred over the centuries helped us get out of there with less digging, my dear Watson," said Wayne. "You have a good point. The hill probably went all of the way down to the lake that is behind us," said Matt.

They turned around and looked at the lake. "Well, there is your blue sky which you were looking at," said Matt. They stood there looking out at the clear blue lake. They located their cars and decided to meet at Stop and Cop in the morning. They drove their cars off into the sunset.

CHAPTER NINE

YOU PUMPKIN HEAD!

Sam stepped out of the bathroom after he made sure all of the mud was cleaned off and stood in front of Mark's door. He heard a slight snore and knew Mark was asleep. Sam opened the door to his bedroom, which was right next to his brothers on the left. He listened to Christian rock music and put his head on the pillow and went into a deep sleep.

It was very dark as Sam looked around in the woods. He looked down to make sure he didn't stray from the path he was following. Then he saw a flash of lightning that lit up the sky. He thought it was too cold for it to rain. He started up on an incline as he continued following the path.

It began to snow very lightly. "That's just great. I'll never find my way out of here," said Sam. The snow began to accumulate, covering the path Sam was following. Sam became confused. "Which way do I go now?" said Sam. He began guessing which way he should go on the path. The tall pine trees were so close together. Sam began thinking he was lost. If I don't get out of here soon, I won't be able to help the guys find the treasure, thought Sam.

Sam came upon what appeared to be a gravestone. Sam knelt down before it. He noticed how small a stone it was as he brushed the snow off the face of it. Well, that is very odd because there isn't a name or date on it. Maybe it is just a stone that looks like a gravestone.

Sam began feeling tired, but he didn't want to fall asleep with the cold and the snow, he felt like he wouldn't wake up. He fought falling asleep, but his eyes became heavy. He couldn't fight it any longer. He fell asleep as the snow continued to fall. Time passed and a mound of snow moved. Sam emerged from the snow yawning and stretching his arms. He looked around and noticed piles of snow surrounding his body. "What is going on here?" asked Sam. He found himself still in the woods. The snow finally stopped and he looked up at the full moon in the sky. He heard a wolf howling in the night. Sam looked down at the gravestone, once more brushing the snow off of it. When he glanced at it, he could not see a name and date this time. The wording was too small to read because the stone appeared to be smaller. He leaned forward to read when he saw his name on it and the dates for being born, 1970 and died 1985. He looked up towards the sky to scream, but nothing came out.

That is when he saw two shadows walk by him on his right. I don't think I imagined that, he thought. He slowly stood up and his joints were stiff from the cold. Moving a little more freely, Sam began to walk quickly, trying to catch up to where he thought the shadows went.

I'll catch up to them. I'll just follow their footprints in the snow. Sam looked down, but he couldn't find any footprints. I am pretty certain I saw them go this way. I must be dreaming, Sam thought. I'll just keep going. Maybe I'll cross paths with them. If I find them, maybe they know the way out of here, Sam thought.

Sam looked straight ahead as far as he could see. Sam saw two objects moving in the far off distance. That must be them. As Sam started to walk faster, he finally put a smile on his face. I'm about to exit this forest once and for all.

The moonlight illuminated the trees. Sam began to see the shadows take shape. I can say one looks like it might be a dog following his master that is wearing a long black cloak with the hood completely covering his head.

Sam heard the wolf again howling in the night. It seemed so much closer. Suddenly, the two figures stopped. They looked straight ahead. Sam wondered why they stopped, perhaps they heard him following them, but didn't turn around, they probably see something I don't see. The pine trees completely obstructed Sam's view and that is when he approached a clearing. Sam looked up and his jaw just dropped in awe.

Sam was looking up at this enormous house. It almost seemed like the house itself extended into the sky.

The shadows didn't move. Sam looked around. He didn't see a way out. Looking at the house, it seemed inviting. I have just about had enough. Since they won't come to me, I will go to them Sam thought. He headed up a steep hill towards what looked like statues. Sam could still see his breath in the cold of the night. He kept rubbing his arms and hitting his legs to keep his circulation going and to keep himself warm.

Sam stopped about ten feet away from them. He noticed it wasn't a dog at all, but an overgrown wolf on steroids. He heard a constant growling from the wolf. Sam began to rationalize that this probably wasn't a good idea. I think I should slowly back up and get out of here as fast as I can thought Sam. If the wolf turns around, he'll be looking for a bone and that bone is buried inside of me.

Sam began to back up slowly when the person in the cloak turned around. This is not good, thought Sam. Sam stopped and froze in his tracks. The person in the cloak was now facing him. The wolf turned around, snarling.

The guys will probably find the treasure without me. A slight tear rolled down Sam's cheek. Sam looked down at the wolf. He looked up at the person in the cloak. It was very dark and he couldn't see anything.

Sam couldn't help himself, when he realized he could speak. "Hey are you the spirit from Christmas past?" laughed Sam. Suddenly, his arm rose and he slowly removed his hood. Sam was rendered speechless. Once the hood was removed it revealed a very hideous skull. It didn't appear human at all. Sam wanted to scream and run, but he couldn't move. It moved towards Sam and extended his right arm straight.

The wolf remained where it was still snarling, and showing his large teeth. Sam extended his left arm and hand. Sam attempted to pull it back, but couldn't because a powerful force seemed to control his movement. A skeletal hand extended from the cloak and Sam cringed. He thought this was the end of his life. When it opened its hand and dropped the object, Sam clenched down on it hard.

It started to laugh very loud. It made a piercing sound while moving towards the house. It seemed like it was floating inches from the ground. Sam started to feel safer now. He remembered the fangs. The wolf wasn't following the thing in the cloak. The wolf ran towards Sam and pounced.

Sam screamed and sat up in his bed perspiring profusely and with his heart rapidly beating. Looking around, he began to calm down and realized that it had been a nightmare. Mark opened Sam's door and asked him what happened. "I thought I heard a girl scream," said Mark. He continued to look at Sam.

Mark looked at Sam. "It must have been some nightmare Sue, I mean Sam," he said. "Laugh it up big guy," said Sam. "You know I will," said Mark.

"Well, anyway, you had better get ready. We have to meet Wayne and Matt at Stop and Cop in

Westminster in a couple of hours. If you are not ready, I'll come in here and pummel you," said Mark.

Mark slammed the door and one could still hear him laughing in the hallway. Sam calmed himself down and noticed his hands were still clenched. He slowly began to open his hands. It was a little painful since they were closed tight for a long period of time. When he finally relaxed, he saw a gold coin in his left one.

Sam calmed himself down and noticed his hands were still clenched. He slowly began to open his hands. It was a little painful since they were closed tight for a long period of time. His hands were finally relaxed when he saw a gold coin in his left one.

CHAPTER TEN

THE ESTATE

Wayne rolled over in his bed and noticed Matt's bed was empty. He thought to himself that his brother was probably downstairs buttering up his parents and covering himself in case anything went wrong. Wayne rolled out of bed and exchanged his pajamas for his jeans and a shirt. He thought it would be great to be like the Stooges and put pajamas on over his clothes.

Wayne went downstairs into the kitchen. "Good morning sleepy head. Are you coming down to join us?" asked Mom. "Well you missed breakfast and I'm not running a restaurant here," said Mom. "I know I'll make my own breakfast," said Wayne. He opened up the cupboard and poured himself a bowl of Apple Jacks. Wayne ate his breakfast in the dining room.

"Now I can see what Matt is up to," said Wayne to himself. He walked into the living room and asked, "Hey Dad how is the estate?" said he. "Well Wayne it is running smooth and on schedule," said Dad. "Glad to hear it, what are you too watching?" asked Wayne. "The Good Bad and the Ugly," said Dad. "It is one of the classic Clint Eastwood movies," said Dad. Wayne sat down on the couch with his brother. "What's up guy? Ready to meet Mark and Sam later?" asked Wayne. "Yeah we are supposed to meet them around eleven or so," said Matt. Dad was sitting upright in his recliner sipping his coffee and reading the newspaper. Mom was sitting on the other side of the living room reading a women's magazine.

"What are you boys up to today?" asked Dad. Wayne and Matt

looked at one another. Wayne hesitated and then said, "We probably will go to the record store with Mark and Sam and then Radio Shack later." "Well, stay away from the mountain today," said Dad. Wayne and Matt glanced at one another again wondering if he knew anything about what they were really up to. "I just saw on the news this morning that a few hikers found some kind of cave up there with human remains. They thought it could be the first settlers," said Dad. "That's really cool Dad. What else did they say?" asked Matt. "They did show an old gold coin," he said. "We must have missed that one," said Wayne. "That's it?" "Nothing else?" asked Wayne. "They didn't say much more, you know the news. It becomes redundant. I shut it off. They probably have reporters, historians and archeologists from all over the country excavating there for a few days," said Dad.

He continued saying, "They think that someone else found the place before the hikers. They located footprints from the person they believed committed the crime," said Dad. "Were you boys up there yesterday?" asked Mom. "Yeah, but we didn't find any cave. We usually find a Native American bow and arrow, but that's about it," said Wayne. "It seems that we never have any luck, not like those two hikers," said Matt. "Maybe someday you boys will find something worthwhile," said Mom. "Yeah right Mom, that's a good one," said Matt.

"Is there anyone watching this movie?" asked Mom. "No, because we have seen it a few times already," said Wayne. "It's boring after you have seen it the first time," said Matt. "Yeah, it's in the script," said Matt. They laughed in unison and Dad turned off the television.

"Well, Mom and Dad, I think we are going to head out," said Wayne. "Keep the estate running smoothly," said Matt. "Keep the light on for us," said Wayne. They exited the room and went outside to the car. Standing at the car, they looked at one another over the roof. "That was a close one," said Wayne. "What now, do we call it off?" asked Matt. "Nobody will ever find out it was us up there. You know how many people go up there every day. It's impossible for anyone to place us in that cave," said Wayne. "You think Mom and Dad will see through us?" asked Matt. "I think that they will look past us and be very happy!" said Wayne. "You are right just like Mom said, maybe we will find something worthwhile," said Matt.

"Let's go because we have a treasure waiting for us," said Wayne. They hopped in the car and sped off into the distance...

CHAPTER ELEVEN

STOP AND COP

They headed down Route 2A towards Westminster. The speedometer on the Chevelle reached 70 miles per hour. Wayne and Matt knew it was smooth sailing. When they saw the big chair on the curve, they knew it was safe. Almost everyone knew where the police would hide and wait to issue tickets. Usually, it was in the parking lot of the garage across from the big chair.

"We are in the clear for now," said Matt. Wayne inserted a Christian rock cassette tape and soon they were driving by Kay's ice cream and sandwich shop. They hit the straight away with swamps on both sides. "Mark and Sam are waiting for us," said Matt. "We mustn't keep them waiting," said Wayne. He accelerated a little and then slowed down as they went over the hill into Westminster. They pulled into the parking lot to Stop and Cop. Mark and Sam were waiting outside. They were sipping on some large ice coffees from Dunkin Donuts.

"Where have you guys been?" asked Mark. "We were caught up in traffic," said Wayne. "Let's go and check out our favorite record store," said Wayne. "Before we do, I think we should figure out the map," said Mark. "Well, Matt and I looked it over half of the night. We know the pine tree in the middle is probably the tallest around. We noticed a cross beside the tree, but we still don't know what that means. We know that there was a very large pine tree down by the football field centuries ago," said Wayne.

"That means we are really out of luck," said Mark. "No, not exactly. We should still check it out before we jump to conclusions," said Wayne.

"Let's go see our buddy Dave in the store," said Wayne. They entered the record store. "Hey, what is up Dave?" asked Wayne. "Stocking some new albums, nothing you boys would listen to," said Dave. "You must mean that soft rock they have out in California," said Mark. "You guessed it, nothing like the Christian rock music," said Wayne.

They came out each carrying a box in both hands. "There's an inch of dust on these boxes," said Dave. "Are you really going to sell these albums?" asked Matt. "I really thought about it and maybe I could sell them to easy listeners," said Dave. "Come on Dave, (as Wayne pulled out a few albums) who really listens to this genre of music anymore?" asked Matt. Wayne continuously slid all of the albums out of the box saying, "There's nothing like Christian rock bands, it's the best music!" said he. "Anyway, boys, if the other easy listening albums don't sell, we'll return all of them to the state of Tennessee," said Dave.

"You boys up to no good today?" asked Dave. "You know us too well, Dave," said Mark. "What is up with your boy over there Sam?" asked Dave. "Sam, he had some sort of nightmare and has been in a trance all morning," said Mark. "You could have fooled me. I always thought that was his normal state," said Matt.

"I'd like to give you the information first," said Dave. "Information, about what?" asked Wayne. "There are all kinds of reporters hanging around and some are questioning me," said Dave. "What are the reporters doing in Westminster in the first place?" asked Mark. "I guess they found some sort of archeological find up at the mountain and a cave with human remains," said Dave.

All of the boys looked at one another. "What sort of questions are they asking you?" asked Matt. "They showed me a picture of a gold coin and asked if anyone accidentally paid me with one. They also wanted to know if I noticed any bizarre behavior from anyone," said Dave. "I told them that I hadn't noticed anything unusual," said Dave. "They said that someone took some valuable artifacts," said Dave.

"They have been here for a few months. People will be coming from all over the country.

Westminster will become a very popular place for a brief time," said Dave. "You should try to avoid that area for a while. You don't want to be caught up there," said Dave, "You know us Dave, we always stay away from trouble," said Matt. "We don't want any trouble so we will have to go underground," laughed Mark.

"What is on the agenda for the rest of the day?" asked Dave. "I think we are going to look for the treasure," said Wayne. "That's a good one Wayne," laughed Dave. Then they looked at one another and began to laugh out loud. "If you boys do find the treasure then you can buy this place, so I can retire in the Bahamas," laughed Dave. "All I can say is that you boys always make me laugh," said Dave. "Well you boys stay safe and don't do anything I wouldn't do," said Dave. "See you next week Dave or maybe sooner," said Wayne. The boys left Stop and Cop.

CHAPTER TWELVE

NERD ALERT!

The boys stood by the cars. "That's good you and Matt knew about this all along and didn't tell us," said Mark. "What do you think was the reason we were late, our parents told us about it. They saw it on the news," said Wayne. "That's just great! Now everyone will be on our heels," said Mark. "That's not necessarily true because no one knows who was actually in the cave in the first place," said Matt. "So, we have that going for us Mark," said Wayne. "Who is going to suspect four teenagers anyway?" asked Matt. "Good point Mark. Are you in or out?" asked Wayne. "I'm still in," said Mark. "How about that guy in a trance over there?" asked Wayne. Mark punched Sam in the arm. "What?" asked Sam. "Are you in or out?" asked Wayne. "I'm in. I'm not a quitter," said Sam. Mark swung and hit him in the arm again. "That's just great, now I can't feel it because it is numb," laughed Sam.

"Now that we are all here mentally and physically, we can get onto the expedition," said Wayne. "Don't turn around now, but we have a historian alert," said Matt. "Excuse me fellas, but I'm here from the Boston Museum of Science. I'm a historian. Here is my card," said he. "What can we do for you Mr.

Stevens?" asked Wayne. "I'm here on an archeological find at the base of the mountain," said Mr. Stevens. "Are you sure that you are in the right place?" asked Matt. "Nothing has been discovered around here," said Matt. "Yes, I'm sure because very early this morning, two hikers stumbled upon a cave," said Mr. Stevens.

"It's the first time that we have heard of it, Mr. Stevens," said Wayne.

"Sorry again, but we are just here to pick up some Christian music," said Mark. "Well, if you hear of anything, you have my card," said Mr. Stevens. "There is just a question of some missing artifacts," said Mr. Stevens. "We will call you if we find anything," said Wayne. Mr. Stevens walked away slightly glancing over his shoulders a few times before entering Dunkin Donuts.

"What a guy!" said Sam. "Do you ever notice how historians wear colors which clash?" asked Matt.

"Now that he has left, we will meet you at the field," said Wayne. Mark and Sam exited the parking lot, smoking the tires on the GTO. Wayne started the Chevelle. The exhaust kicked up Mr. Stevens' card as the wind took it away. Wayne and Matt followed them down Main Street. They waved to Mr. Stevens through the window.

While driving towards the high school, Mark hit his brakes because he noticed a police cruiser. The police officer was watching them and he smiled. Matt returned the smile and the police officer gave them a nod and drove away. Wayne looked back in the rear-view mirror as the cruiser disappeared over the hill.

Wayne made it a rule to always smile at a police officer in an effort to show respect. He knew when they saw a muscle car, it is almost a guaranteed speeding ticket. It is the reason why Wayne kept an eye out for the police. Wayne affixed a slogan to the back of the vehicle which reads support your local and state police. Wayne thought that it would help if he or the others were ever pulled over by the police.

"Well, we are in the clear. It is smooth sailing from here," said Wayne. "What if that guy returns to us and asks questions?" asked Mark. "I guess that we will cross that bridge when it comes," said Wayne.

They drove a few more miles out to the football field. Wayne followed Mark through the parking lot.

Mark dove to the far left of the lot until he reached a grassy hill. Wayne parked close to his vehicle. They exited the vehicles and looked up at all of the tall pines.

CHAPTER THIRTEEN

THE FOREST

"I guess we are in business again," said Wayne. "How are we even going to find this tree?" asked Mark. "On the map it shows the tree in the middle and small trees around it," said Wayne. "So it must be the tallest of the trees. It shouldn't be too hard to find," said Wayne. "That is easier said than done," said Sam.

"This treasure hunt is becoming further away from us," said Matt. "It has been centuries, maybe someone happened to come upon it and found the treasure," said Matt. "If that were true, we would have heard about it in our history class," said Wayne. "Another valid point, my dear Watson," said Matt.

"Let's go and check it out and if we can't find it then we will call it quits," said Wayne. "'Agreed?" asked Wayne. They shouted "Onward and Upward" as Wayne pointed to the hill.

They passed several tree stumps as they walked up the hill. "Well there's your answer, someone cut it down," said Sam. "Let's not give up yet," said Matt. They came upon the outskirts of the pine forest. "If we enter it we may not come back out alive," laughed Wayne. "I don't know about you guys, but I don't scare too easily," said Mark. Mark led the way and one by one they followed him into the dark abyss, now knowing the outcome.

They travelled deeper into the forest looking at the size of the trees. There was a very brief moment of laughter when all of a sudden, they heard twigs snapping behind them. "What was that?" asked Matt. "I think someone is following us," said Mark. "Well, whoever it is we will just tell him that we are doing some exploring," said Wayne.

"I can still hear something moving out there," said Sam. They stood still when a fox scurried by them.

They looked at one another and burst into laughter. "Well at least it wasn't big foot," laughed Mark. "My heart was beating so fast. I thought this was it," said Matt. "Mine too," said Wayne.

"Let's look further ahead," said Mark. "Wait, hold up guys," said Matt as the laughter faded away. "We are getting no place fast! I think that we should all split up," said Matt. "Yeah, Matt has a point because we are just going around in circles," said Wayne. "You Sam, take the right, Mark to the left and me and Matt will split off straight ahead," said Wayne. "If anything should happen or you find something, just yell and we will all come running," said Wayne.

CHAPTER FOURTEEN

YOU GO YOUR WAY AND I'LL GO MINE

The four boys split up, disappearing into the forest, now knowing what would occur. Sam continuously reassured himself that he was not afraid. He was thinking about what he was getting himself into on this expedition. He was worried because when he was with the others, he received the worst of it. "I want to turn the table around on those guys, find the treasure and end this charade. This way I won't have to look over my shoulder all of the time!" he said to himself. "Relax, there is nothing to be afraid of here," said Sam.

Sam looked up at the pine trees. "Man, I'll have to get a chiropractor once this is all said and done. This is silly, looking for the tallest tree in the forest, especially, when they all look the same," he said to himself. He wanted to return to the car and leave it all up to the rest of the guys.

Sam stopped and listened. It was quiet, almost too quiet. "Those guys better not play any tricks on me. Knowing them, they returned to their cars and left," he spoke to himself. Sam did not hear any cars in the distance. "I know that they didn't leave me here," Sam said to himself. "I would have heard the engines of those muscle cars," he said.

It was very quiet for the woods. Sam didn't even hear the birds chirping, not even the squirrels. He began to wonder why he didn't hear anything. "Maybe there is a bear or mountain lion out there," he said to himself. Sam moved forward deeper into the forest and still nothing caught his eye. Sam began to hear faint voices in the distance, but couldn't decipher the words.

He hesitated going forward, but he was curious. "It is just probably some punks partying out here, and if so, I'm out of here," he thought. Sam stopped behind a tree when he looked around it and rubbed his eyes because he couldn't believe what he was seeing. He glanced at it again and saw a large fire with Native Americans surrounding it. They wore feathers in their hair and war paint. They appeared to be very angry. They seemed vigilant and Sam noticed that there weren't many in number.

They spoke to one another and Sam thought that it was his turn to slowly retreat without being detected. One of the Native Americans looked at the fire and saw something shiny like a large gold medallion. As soon as it appeared, it was gone. Sam leaned forward when he was noticed. Sam stared at the Native American. His image was frightening to Sam. He thought that it had to be the war paint.

Sam slowly backed away when the Native American picked up a spear and threw it. The spear quickly embedded itself in the tree. It was a few inches from Sam's head. Sam screamed at the top of his lungs running as fast as possible.

Sam ran and called for the others and he looked back to see if anyone was chasing him, but all he was able to see were the trees. "I think that I am in the clear now," said Sam. Sam turned and tripped over a rock skinning his hands. He noticed that they were scraped and bloody. Sam thought about what Wayne said about not returning alive. "Mark, Wayne, Matt!" he screamed. "Where are you?" said Sam. He tried to stand, but his knees were badly wounded. He knew he had to get up and run. Sam fought through the unbearable pain. As he stood up, he found that he couldn't run that fast anymore.

"I'm going to make it out of here with or without the guys," he said to himself. Sam yelled for the guys in each direction. Sam looked around, but nothing looked familiar. "I can't spend a night in these woods, because the natives are restless," Sam thought.

Sam decided to ascend the hill. "Maybe there is a clearing up ahead and I can get my bearings and make my escape," Sam thought. Sam looked up into the sky, making sure the sun wasn't too low. Sam brought his flashlight in case it became too dark.

"I'm all alone!" said Sam. "No, you are not. I'm here with you," said Wayne. "Are you trying to give me a heart attack?" said Sam. "Chill, I heard you yelling, so I came as fast as I could," said Wayne. "What took you so long? I've been screaming for one half of an hour!" said Sam. "I was half way up the hill when I heard you yelling," said Wayne.

Mark and Matt came running. "What was all of the yelling about?" asked Mark. "I think your brother here saw his shadow," laughed Wayne. Sam pushed himself up once again, still feeling the scrapes and bruises. "What happened to you dude?" asked Matt. "I was running when I tripped over a rock," said Sam. "What were you running, from a chipmunk?" asked Matt. "I think if I told you, you would probably think that I'm crazy," said Sam. "You can try us, what did you see?" asked Wayne.

"Well, I came upon a clearing when I heard voices, so I looked around the tree and saw a fire with a few Native Americans gathered around it. One of them threw a spear at me and missed and that is when I took off running," said Sam. They looked at one another in disbelief. "Don't believe me, but I saw it and I'm telling you the truth," said Sam. "It's not that, but even at the farmhouse I started seeing weird things along with the nightmare I had last night," said Sam.

"Something is not right here guys and I think you feel it too," said Sam. Looking at one another they shrugged their shoulders. "Maybe we do feel a strange vibe since we began this crazy expedition," said Wayne. "But I'm willing to fight for all its worth," said Wayne. "If there is any danger, we will make a quick escape and never look back," said Wayne. "Is that alright with you Sam or do you want to quit?" asked Wayne. "We can still make this happen with the three of us," said Wayne. "Really? And let you three get all of the glory," said Sam. "I'll hang in there, but if it really becomes too dangerous, I'm out," said Sam. "Great, now we can move onward and upward," said Wayne.

CHAPTER FIFTEEN

LOST YET FOUND

"Let's head up to the top of the hill because there might be a clearing or even a tree up there," said Wayne. They began ascending the hill and stopped for a few water breaks. "I think that I see the clearing up ahead," said Matt. Glancing upward at the top of the trees, "I still don't see a pine tree in the forest," said Mark. "I see several more stumps scattered about," said Sam. "Hey guys! Come up here. I found a small shack," yelled Wayne. They stared at the boarded- up shack. "It doesn't look like a pine tree to me," said Sam. "Let's check it out anyway," said Wayne.

They stood on the porch, hoping it would support all of their weight. When Wayne pushed on the door, it fell to the floor. They kicked the dust as they walked inside. "It looks like a one room shack," said Matt. "I don't see anything in here," said Mark. "Well, it was worth checking out," said Wayne.

They exited the shack and sat down on the porch. They held their heads and felt bad that they had traveled this far for only a few coins. "Now we have come to a dead end," said Mark. "Yeah, I guess you are right guys. I guess we were just deceiving ourselves," said Wayne. "So let it be written, so let it be done!" Mark saw the horizon above the trees. The sun was becoming low and soon it would be dark. He looked at the football field. He glanced past the field and saw it. His pupils were dilated and he was excited. 'Guys!" yelled Mark. "I see it! I see it!" screamed Mark. They were startled by Mark's excitement. Mark pointed his finger straight ahead. They all followed his lead, but didn't see anything. "What are you looking at?" asked Wayne. "Down past the football field it is the tree for which we have been searching," said Mark. They noticed it was the tallest tree that they had ever seen. It towered over all of the other trees. They jumped for joy. "Mark you found it!" they screamed with excitement.

They calmed down and rationalized the situation. "Let's head down there before it becomes dark," said Mark. They patted Mark on the back and walked through the woods to their cars on the other side of the field. "I think it looked like it was about fifty yards in," said Mark. "Out of the woods into another," said Sam. They took out their flashlights as they entered the woods.

They looked up until they came to the tree. They followed it all the way down to the ground. "That is one tall tree. It must be at least three to four hundred feet tall," said Wayne. "The base of this tree has to be at least thirty feet around," said Matt. "First question guys, what are we looking for?" asked Sam. "Good question. Let's look at the map once again," said Wayne. Wayne pulled out the map and opened it up. They shined their lights on it, studying the map. "All I can see out of the ordinary is this cross next to the tree," said Matt. "It looks like it was a red cross at the time. The color is faded," said Wayne. "We must be looking for some sort of cross around the tree," said Matt. Wayne closed the map and put it away. They circled the tree looking for the cross. They made a point of searching several feet away from the tree.

"Find anything guys?" asked Wayne. "No, maybe we are not looking in the right area," said Matt. "It might be made out of sticks or stones," said Wayne. "Yeah, but I don't even see it," said Sam. "Let's take a break guys, we aren't making any progress at all," said Matt.

They sat down on a rock close nearby and Wayne leaned his hand against the tree. I guess we are all in limbo once again," said Mark. "I wish it would have a sign saying here is the treasure, spend wisely," said Matt. "l say we get the shovels which we brought with us and start digging around the tree," said Sam.

"Brilliant! You dig for the buried treasure," said Mark. "I don't know. I think we are missing something and it is not digging," said Wayne. "Let's just go home and sleep on it and start fresh in the morning," said

Matt. "Yeah, you are right. We are all tired and not thinking straight," said Mark.

"Let's get out of here and start fresh tomorrow," said Wayne. They stood up and Wayne took his hand off the tree. "That's just great! I have sap all over my hand," said Wayne. Wayne looked down at his hand. "This isn't right. I have red sap all over my hand," said Wayne. Wayne glanced back at the tree. He noticed a red streak from the base of the tree as far as he could see. "Guys come over here and flash your lights up the tree. I think one of us should climb it," said Wayne. "Not me," said Matt.

Then they looked at Sam. "I guess that you are the lucky candidate," said Wayne. "Oh no, not me guys. I'll break my neck if I fall," said Sam. "We will catch you if you fall," said Matt. "That's some insurance trusting you guys to catch me," said Sam. "I'll boost you up to the nearest limb so you can climb up and find the source of the red sap," said Wayne.

"This is just great! Why do I have to do all of the climbing?" asked Sam. "You are like a spider monkey when it comes to trees," said Mark. "Okay, I'll do it, but I won't like it," said Sam.

Wayne leaned up against the tree. Sam climbed onto his shoulders. Wayne boosted Sam up until he grabbed onto one of the limbs. "That a girl, I mean boy, climb that tree," said Matt. Sam began climbing the branches one by one very slowly. "Don't look down. Keep looking up!" said Mark. Sam seized the next branch climbing and it seemed like there wasn't an end to the red sap.

"You find anything up there yet?" asked Mark. "Nothing yet, I'm still climbing," yelled Sam. "I can barely see him up there," said Wayne. "Keep climbing, you are doing well," said Matt. "Keep climbing, he says, how about you climb it," said Sam. Sam took a break, glancing up into the darkness. Sam held onto the next branch and heard a crack underneath him. He made sure to be very careful the rest of the way.

Sam ascended a few more branches and looked at the tree to see if he had to go any further. He was focused on the cross that they were searching for. "Hey guys, I found the cross!" yelled Sam. "All this time we were looking for it down here when it was up there," said Mark. Sam looked over the cross, examining it. "That is strange, someone carved out a square and sealed it up with the sap. It was probably painted red or even with blood for that matter. It just wore off with the sap dripping and the rain," said Sam.

Sam traced all four sides with his finger. "Maybe just maybe, they carved a clue on the backside of the cross," said Sam. Sam reached in his pocket and took out his pocket knife. He opened the blade and started cutting the sap that sealed it for centuries. When he felt it loosen, he began prying on it until it extended out. Sam clamped his hands on it so he wouldn't drop it down on anyone's head. He turned the cross around to look on the backside. "Nothing, absolutely nothing, and suddenly, something caught Sam's eyes. Looking back in the hole, he grabbed onto a large medallion. Sam thought about what he saw in the fire a while ago. He remembered it was a large medallion just like this one.

Sam looked the medallion over noticing what looked like a small island and on the other side a small boat. Sam put it in his pocket, took a leather satchel that was also inside the hole and slid it back into his pocket.

"I'm dropping down the cross," he said. Sam dropped it on the ground. Sam began to descend the tree.

He took a deep breath. "I could have plummeted to my untimely demise," he thought. Sam literally hung from the last branch, dropping to the ground. "Great job Sam! What did you find up there?" asked Wayne. "Well, I found another satchel and probably another map. In addition, I found a gold medallion," said Sam. Sam laid them down on a nearby rock. "Let's see what our next quest will be," said Wayne.

Deciphering the map, it gave a list of coordinates without an X marking the spot this time. The shape in the middle looked like three triangles. Matt pointed out that it had to be on an island. Matt continued to show the medallion. "All I see here are many rocks and trees. The map doesn't give us much of a clue and neither does the medallion. This has been a wild goose chase," said Mark.

"Let's look at the island again," said Wayne. "Matt, doesn't the island look familiar?" asked Wayne. "Isn't that the island we built a fort on in the winter?" asked Matt. "Bingo! That's exactly the same one, almost practically right in our back yard," said Wayne.

"What are you two talking about?" asked Mark. "Behind our back yard is the farmer's field. One winter we built this ramp out of snow on the hill. We put water on it and froze it overnight. We took our sled and went down the hill: We would hit the ramp and get lots of air; except, you had to grip very hard onto the sled because once you hit the ground, you either lost control or would slide right onto the frozen pond onto the island. Once we knew the ice was safe, we would cross onto the island and build a fort on it," said Wayne.

"It's wild we were on that island the whole winter, not knowing there was a treasure," said Matt. "That's just great guys, but if this is the island you are talking about then this map and medallion doesn't give us much of a clue," said Mark. "That's all we have to go on right now. Maybe once we get onto the island, we might stumble upon something," said Matt. "Let's get out of here and worry about it tomorrow," said Sam. "We will meet you at your house around noon," said Mark. "Sounds like a plan, now, let's get out of here!" Retrieving the three items, Wayne put them in his backpack. They walked back to the cars and Wayne said "See you tomorrow dudes." The rear lights to the cars faded away into the darkness...

CHAPTER SIXTEEN

TOMORROW'S LECTURE

Matt sat on the side of his bed. Wayne rolled over looking at Matt. "What's wrong? Why aren't you downstairs?" he asked. "We returned last night around two-thirty, don't you think they are down there waiting for us, so they can give us another lecture?" asked Matt. "Don't worry, they will get over it. They always do," said Wayne. "You can always side track Dad by asking him about sports, but Mom, not so much," said Wayne.

"Well, let's go down and get it over with," said Matt. Wayne and Matt made it down into the kitchen. They saw Dad in the living room having his coffee and reading the newspaper in his recliner. "Hey Dad, how is the estate this morning?" asked Wayne. "Where were you two boys last night?" he asked with a stern look on his face. "We were over Mark's studying for future exams," said Wayne. "You expect me to believe a story like that. I don't and I know that your mother won't either," said Dad. "You wouldn't believe us if we told you anyway," said Matt. "Try me, but I'm sure it is another lie," said Dad.

"Well, we found these maps and were hunting for treasure," said Wayne. "It is another foolish treasure hunt. You played those games when you were kids. It's about time you four grew up. Before you know it, life will hit you right in the face, and here you boys are looking at a fake map," said Dad. "Go outside and talk to your mother in the garden," said Dad. He returned to reading his newspaper.

"See that wasn't so bad. It could have been worse," said Wayne. "I thought you were going to do that sports thing with him," said Matt.

"I didn't think there was a need to," said Wayne. They exited the house and walked out to the garden. Mom was picking some ripe tomatoes and green beans. "You boys see your father," said Mom. "Yeah, he let us have it," said Wayne. "You boys should know better than to have us worry where you are," said Mom. "If you are near a phone, call us and tell us you will be late and that you are safe," said Mom. "We are sorry Mom. We will do that next time," said Wayne and Matt.

"Because next time you might be grounded," said Mom. "Now, I'm busy, you two are off the hook this time," said Mom. "That was a close one," said Matt. "At least we didn't have to make our escape plan," said Wayne. They sat down on the picnic table waiting for Mark and Steve. Mom walked by heading into the house. "Invite your friends overnight for a barbecue we are having," said Mom. "It sounds great. Thanks Mom," said Wayne. She went into the house. "At least we can enjoy food and friends tonight," said Matt. "Yeah, we need a break," said Wayne.

"What if what Dad said was right, that we are looking for treasure that really isn't there?" asked Matt. "I admit when we were little, we drew treasure maps, played with baseball cards, quarters, pennies, even an old television guide, but Matt this is different. We are not kids anymore and we didn't create these treasure maps," said Wayne.

"We found those maps and I believe this treasure is real. We are the only ones who really know about it," said Wayne. "I'll have to admit the maps do look authentic and the coins are real," said Matt. "Exactly, so why would you doubt it? Let's find the treasure and become famous," said Wayne. "I'm with you, but where are the other two?" asked Matt.

"I think I hear them pulling into the driveway," said Wayne. Mark and Sam came around the back of the house. They sat down at the picnic table. "Where were you guys?" asked Wayne. "I had to get my beauty sleep," laughed Sam. "We were lectured last night by our parents," said Mark. "We were lectured as well this morning," said Matt.

"I thought about the island last night. Neither one of us have a boat," said Mark. "Yeah and I can't swim," said Matt. "Alright, the farmer has an aluminum row boat which he allows us to borrow from time to time," said Wayne. "Well, let's stop procrastinating and get on with this hunt," said Wayne.

They headed towards the farmer's field and jumped over a stone wall. "Yeah, guys our parents invited you two for our barbecue tonight," said Wayne. "It sounds great. I can't wait because your Mom is such a great cook," said Mark. "Thanks," said Wayne.

They made it to the old rickety barn where the boat was housed. Wayne yelled to Mr. and Mrs. Shepard. "We are going to borrow the boat for a while," said Wayne. They were both in their rocking chairs on the porch of their house. Mr. Shepard waved. "Just looking at those two reminds me of a Norman Rockwell painting," said Matt. "That's great Matt, but pick up an end of the boat. You two carry the oars," said Wayne. They walked down the hill to the shore line. They looked across the water to the small island. "That is the magnificent island you two were talking about," said Mark. "It will be great if we find the treasure over there and then you can call it anything you want," said Wayne. "I'm not climbing up any tree this time," said Sam. "If anyone has to climb a tree, I will," said Wayne.

CHAPTER SEVENTEEN

THE ISLAND

"Let's all get into the boat. Matt and I will row. It can't be more than fifty yards," said Wayne. They set out for another adventure not knowing what the island held. "I think I'm finally getting this rowing down," said Matt. "I could be one of the fastest rowers in the world," laughed Matt. "There are some ducks in this pond," said Mark. "Yeah, and I hope they don't dive bomb us either," said Sam. "We are about half way there. Look up there is a hawk circling the island," said Wayne. "He probably has his nest there or he is hunting for lunch," said Mark. "I bet there are tons of fish in here. We should have brought our fishing poles," said Sam. "There isn't any time for fishing right now, please concentrate on finding this treasure Sam," said Wayne. "Hey guys, we are approaching the shore. They exited in shallow water and pulled the boat ashore. "We have reached our destination," said Mark. "See the great fort we made," said Matt. They studied it for a moment. "I see a few two by fours nailed to the trees," said Mark. "You know some envious person had to destroy it," said Wayne. "Let's get on with the search guys," said Matt.

"Let's get on with the search guys," said Matt. "First off, what are we looking for?" said Mark. "Well, that is the million- dollar question," said Wayne. "Let's look at the map once more and that medallion," said Matt. They studied the map again for several minutes. "The map only shows those three triangles. The medallion shows an island with pine, elm, birch trees and rocks," said Sam.

"We should split up and look around," said Wayne. They separated and searched, not knowing what they would encounter. Wayne found a rope and tied it to a tree that led into the water. He bent down to pull the rope, but there was nothing at the end. "Well if the treasure was there it is long gone," said Wayne. He continued to search the rest of the island.

Sam looked up towards the trees. "All I see is a few bird's nests, nothing that stands out here," said Sam. Sam managed to get his feet entangled in a fishing line. Sam began to unravel it when he was pricked by a hook. "That's just great, my hands aren't even healed from last night's disaster," said Sam.

Mark kicked the leaves around on the ground. He thought to himself that perhaps he would find a clue which would lead him to the treasure. He hoped the end of the hunt would be soon so he could return home.

Matt began kicking over small rocks. He wondered how he could concentrate on a treasure when a barbecue awaited him. I've kicked several rocks, but have not found the treasure. What, is it is all a hoax? he thought. They returned to the middle of the island. "You guys find anything?" asked Wayne. "I didn't find anything at all," said Mark. "I completely searched the area, but didn't find anything. If it were here, it would have been found centuries ago," said Sam.

Matt walked away and looked into the water. "You can see everything from here and I don't see any sign of triangles," said Matt. Sam joined Matt to look out into the water. "Well that really is strike two guys, one more and we are out," said Mark.

"I'm going to look around once more," said Wayne. Wayne pushed off from the rock and cut his hand. "I cut myself on the rock. Be careful Mark not to cut yourself on those sharp points and the rock," said Wayne. "You alright?" asked Mark. "It is a little cut. I think I will survive," said Wayne. "Did you just say what I thought you said?" asked Matt. "Yeah, this rock is dangerous," said Wayne. Matt turned to Wayne and Mark on the rock. "Guys! Get over here now!" said Matt. "I think we found the treasure," said Matt. "Look at the rock from here. There are your three triangles," said Matt. "What made you look at the rock?" asked Sam. "I heard Wayne mention the rock was extremely pointed and the triangles have points, so I put two and two together man. That's really it!" said Matt.

CHAPTER EIGHTEEN

THE ROCK

"Let's go and check out exactly what we did find," said Wayne. "All I see is a rock," said Wayne. They walked over to look at it. "Maybe the triangles are pointing up towards something," said Sam. They looked up and saw a clearing through the trees. "I see a clear blue sky, it must be something else," said Matt. "It could just be a coincidence that the rock had three triangles," said Mark.

"Why don't we start by clearing the debris around it," said Wayne. They took out some shovels which they brought from the boat and quickly cleared out ten feet from the rock. "I really don't see anything except dirt," said Sam. They found themselves on all fours looking around the ground. "Look, I found an engraving on the rock," said Sam. "'It is three triangles upside down. This must be our clue from the map," said Sam. They stared at it. "I don't see any treasure," said Matt. They stood up from the ground, brushing all the loose dirt off of themselves.

"Now that we have located the triangles, what do they really tell us?" said Mark. "I think we are all in the same boat," said Wayne. Sam took out his pocket knife, opening the blade and scraping it against the rock. "What are you doing Sam?" asked Matt. "I thought if I scrape the rock, it might have some gold underneath," said Sam. "It's just a rock," said Sam. "Good one, my dear Watson," said Matt. "Well, you guys have any better ideas?" asked Sam.

"I have it guys! The triangles point downward. I say that the treasure is underneath the rock," said Wayne. "Yeah, underground man," said

Mark. "I have a question, how are we going to budge that large rock or lift it for that matter?" asked Sam. "Let me think about it," said Wayne. No one said a word. "My brilliant mind has come up with something that just might work," said Wayne.

"What could that be genius?" asked Mark. "I say that we get three good size rocks even if it takes all four of us to bring them over and then use the smaller rocks for leverage. The fourth guy will try to push it over while the other three lift the rock with the two by fours," said Wayne.

"Brilliant!" yelled Matt. "Thank you," said Wayne. "Let's go retrieve the rocks and the rest of the equipment," said Wayne. "Now that we took a short rest from carrying those heavy rocks. We are all set up and we dug under the rock for the three two by fours. So, on the count of three, you three pull down on the two by fours by lifting the rock and I'll push with all of my might to push it over," said Wayne. "Okay, Hercules, let's do this," said Mark.

"One, two, three, lift.... She's a heavy one," said Matt. "The rock is beginning to move," said Wayne. "I think it is my time to start pushing on it. Bear down on those two by fours. She is going. The rock finally flipped on its side. It made a huge crash to the ground. We did it guys! It raised my blood pressure, but we did it," yelled Wayne.

"At least we didn't have to blast this time," said Matt. "Sometimes it is hard to be one of the most brilliant men in the world," said Wayne. They stood around in a circle where the rock used to be. "Itlooks like we will have to dig," said Mark. They picked up the shovels and started to dig. "I thought moving the rock raised my blood pressure," said Wayne. "I didn't think there would be so much labor involved," said Matt.

One hour passed and the boys had dug down four feet and five feet around the rock. "If this is someone's idea of a sick joke, I've had enough," said Sam. "If we keep digging the hole, it will probably start filling up with water. We are on an island," said Mark. "Good observation Sherlock," said Wayne. "I'm beginning to lose interest in this expedition," said Matt. "In a few more hours your parents will be looking for us to attend the barbecue tonight," said Mark. "I really don't want to miss hot dogs and hamburgers," said Matt.

"Why don't we dig another foot? If we don't find anything, at least we gave it another try," said Wayne. "Still nothing! I'm out of here," said Sam. Sam threw his shovel in frustration hitting the bottom of the rock knocking some dirt away. "Look Sam you broke the shovel in half, now go and pick it up and put it in the boat," said Matt. Sam went over to retrieve the pieces and knelt down noticing something peculiar about the bottom of the rock.

He began brushing the dirt away. "Sam get the equipment, we are out of here," said Wayne. "Hey Sam! Did you hear me?" asked Wayne. "Pack it up you pumpkin head," said Matt. Wayne went over to get Sam when he saw the bottom of the rock. He stood there speechless.

Matt and Mark stood by the boat, looking forward to the barbecue. "Let's go and get it before the vultures do," said Mark. They went over to wake them up out of a trance. "Come on guys, we don't have all day," said Mark. They stood there looking at the rock in awe.

Wayne rubbed his eyes, not believing what he was seeing, patting Sam on the shoulder several times. "You did it Sam. I'm proud of you. I take back whatever those guys said about you," said Wayne. "We looked everywhere and even dug a huge hole and most of all even worked up a sweat," said Matt. "Exactly, and all along it was the rock," said Mark.

"It's not exactly the treasure, but it is one step closer," said Wayne. "What extraordinary engraving even lining up with the gold," said Sam. "This is our next map and another clue," said Mark. "Look at the magnificent detail on the little man in the middle," said Sam. "We will have to chisel that out. I think it is our next clue," said Wayne. "I'm on it," said Sam.

"We know it is the Quabbin Reservoir with the shape of the large lake. This appears to be a wall of some sort," said Matt. "There are a lot of granite cliffs over there," said Mark. "Maybe this is what they are showing here," said Mark "We can start there first," said Wayne. "Let's get to the barbecue," said Matt. "Yeah, but shouldn't we flip over the rock to hide the map?" asked Sam. "l don't think we have to worry about anyone coming over here," said Mark. "Even if they did, I wouldn't think they were looking at a treasure map," said Matt. "I'm ready to get off this rock," said Mark. "Good one dude, we are off to the barbecue!" said Wayne.

CHAPTER NINETEEN

THE BARBECUE

"Here comes the boys," said Dad. "You boys better wash up because you all look like you crawled out from underneath a rock," said Mom. "After you wash up, take all of the food on the kitchen counter and bring it out here on the table," said Mom. "I also know how much food we have, so don't press your luck," laughed Mom. "Wayne you can cook all of the hamburgers, hot dogs and barbecue the chicken on the grill," said Dad.

"I'm on it, you know that I barbecue the best in the world," said Wayne. "You boys sit yourself down at the table and try some of the salads," said Mom. They helped themselves to the potato, macaroni and tossed salad. "You make the greatest food ever," said Mark. "Thank you Mark, but I'm sure your mother does too," said Mom. "Yeah, she's a great cook," said Mark.

"Everything is on the grill, so let's eat," said Wayne. He placed a large plate on the table with all of the grilled food. They generously loaded their plates. "Wow, you boys are really hungry tonight," said Mom. "Yeah, you boys didn't crawl out of a hole, you probably dug it the way your plates are piled," said Dad.

"Dad, I guess you could say that," said Matt. They looked at one another. "Dad, are you spying on us?" asked Wayne. "I wouldn't put it past you boys not destroying something in a day," said Dad. How do you boys like the barbecue?" asked Mom. They looked at Mom, but their mouths were full. "I think there is your answer," said Dad. "It looks like everything is devoured except for the lonely tossed salad over here," said Dad. "We can wrap that up and save it for tomorrow," said Mom.

"Another great barbecue from the great estate," said Wayne. They thanked Mom and Dad and stood up from the table. When Wayne stood up the golden man fell out of his back pocket and onto the ground. Dad picked it up and asked, "Wayne where did you get this?" to which Wayne responded, "We found it down by the ball field. It feels a little heavy. It isn't gold is it?" asked Dad.

"We thought that it was a steel structure, something that was painted gold," said Wayne. "You boys aren't in some kind of trouble?" asked Dad. "Trouble is what we try to stay away from Dad," said Wayne.

"This doesn't have anything to do with what they found up at the mountain?" asked Dad. "Because if it is you better go right up there and tell them before they come and find you," said Dad. "Calm down Dad, it is really nothing to worry about," said Wayne.

"In the end, Dad, you will be very proud of us," said Wayne. "I just don't want anyone to be hurt," said Dad. "Trust us Dad, we will steer clear of any trouble," said Matt. "I'm telling you boys not to look into this any further," said Dad. "That is the end of the conversation," said Dad.

They cleaned up after the barbecue. Mom and Dad were in for the night. The boys hung outside at the picnic table. "I don't know about you, but when our Dad picked that statue up, I was shocked," said Wayne. "I think all of us felt the same," said Mark. "Maybe your Dad is right, we could be in over our heads here with the treasure," said Sam.

"We can't stop now. I think that we are closer than ever," said Wayne. "Let's put it this way. We will all sleep on it. I know that I'm going to the Quabbin tomorrow," said Wayne. "Whoever else is going might want to bring climbing gear," said Wayne. They agreed to it and finished the day playing baseball in the back yard.

CHAPTER TWENTY
GONE FISHING

There was a little motor boat gliding over the water carrying two fishermen. "Thank God we are starting early enough to go fishing," said John. "Yeah, but four in the morning is a little crazy," said Carl.

"It is hard to get my beauty sleep on the weekends with you," said Carl. "You should be used to it Carl. We go fishing every weekend," said John. "My wife awakens with the phone ringing in her ear. It was three- thirty this morning. "You want to know what she said when I told her who it was?" asked Carl. don't think I want to hear the answer, but go ahead," said John. "She told me you need to get a life," said Carl.

"l like my freedom," said John. "Well, I like my sleep," said Carl. "The island is coming up and here is our hot spot for fishing," said John. "Well, drop the anchor mate, we are coming ashore," laughed Carl. John looked up at him and said "I'm sorry man, but you do need more sleep," said John. "Well, captain, you can help me pull the boat up on shore," said John. "I'll help you, but if I break a nail, I'll never talk to you again," laughed Carl.

"As soon as we do, we can start fishing for bass," said John. They you can take the fish home and cook it up with some eggs and bacon," said John. "Mm bacon, you have to love those pork products," said Carl. "You grab your fishing gear and then begin a beautiful day fishing," said John.

"I'm going over here to fish. I caught a few last time," said John. "I'll fish by the boat," said Carl. John sat down on a rock casting out his line into the water. "Those night crawlers don't catch a fish, nothing else will," said John. He took a ginger ale out of his cooler and took a sip, placing it by his side while waiting for a bite. "I have all of the patience in the world, fish you take the work and you will be all done. I will reel you in and you will be all mine," said John.

"I'm wearing camouflaged clothes just for you," said John. "My friend over there didn't wear camouflaged clothes and will stick out like a sore thumb. He'll be lucky if he catches anything today," said John.

Carl retrieved a soda and set it aside. He cast out his line as he dipped it in the water. "Now I can lean against the tree and let the worm do all of the work," said Carl. "I guess it's true what they say a bad day fishing is better than a good day at work," said Carl. Fishing under the beautiful sun and admiring all of God's creation, it is simply divine," said Carl. "If I didn't have to eat and drink water to survive, I would sit right here and watch the sunrise and the sunset. At night, I would just watch the moon and the stars; except my wife would be wondering where I was and what I was doing. I guess that it is back to reality," said Carl.

Carl watched his bobber move under the water. "Man, I think I have a bite," he thought. He quietly picked up his fishing pole and waited. He felt that he caught something with the weight at the end of the line. He slowly reeled in the fish. He pulled it up on the shore and took the hook out of the big bass. He placed it in the cooler with ice which was in the boat.

"Hey John, I caught a big bass. How about you?" asked Carl. "Nothing yet, I'm still waiting for my first bite," said John. "Today is my lucky day," said Carl. "That's just great," said John. John became discouraged. "I've always had better luck than Carl," he said to himself. "I know it's the worm. I'll change the worm on the line and try once more," said John.

He reeled in the line and placed a fresh worm on the hook. He cast out the line much further this time in the water. "I've always used a worm. I'm old school and it has never failed me," said John. "I'll just wait a little while longer. If I don't catch anything, I'll move my operation on the other side of the island," he said.

John had enough. He could only hear that Carl had caught another one. "Hey Carl, I'm going over to the other side of the island," he said. "Good luck!" yelled Carl. "I thought I was the best fisherman in the world and now Carl is trying to take my place! I can't let that happen," he said.

I hope that I can catch up and pass him at the new spot, he thought. A hawk swooped down on John. He tried to squat down at the last second. John looked up at the hawk, but the sun blinded his view for a few seconds. "You do that once again and I will have you with my bacon tomorrow morning," he said. He continued to walk, not paying attention and fell into a deep hole in the ground. Why me? All I wanted was to have a peaceful and prosperous day fishing, he thought. "Carl! Carl! He yelled. "Right over here, please get me out of this hole!" yelled John.

"How did you get into that hole without seeing it?" asked Carl. "Never mind, just get me out!" said

John. Carl reached down and grabbed onto his hand, pulling him out of the hole. "Thanks man," said John. "Hey John, this hole wasn't here last week," said Carl. "Who came into our sector and dug this hole?" asked Carl. "Probably some meddling kids," said John.

"Well, I'm ready to return fishing. I was on a hot streak man until I heard you," said Carl. "Go and return to your fishing. I'm going over here," said John. "What's wrong now man, you are beginning to stutter on me," said Carl. "Look at the rock Carl. It looks like gold," said John. Carl looked with his eyes wide open. "Those kids probably painted the rock gold," said John. "No Carl, there are really gold flakes. We are rich man! Let's melt it down to some nuggets," said John. "Even if we did, we wouldn't get much for it," said Carl.

John stood back for a moment, looking at the rock. "It is the Quabbin, I'm sure of it. I think we have some kind of treasure map here Carl," said John. "The treasure is very good." "Where can we find this treasure map?" asked Carl. "I wonder if this has anything to do with what they found up there at the mountain," said John. "Yeah, man, I saw that on the news," said Carl.

"If it is, they have a jump on us and they probably found whatever it was," said John. "It wouldn't hurt to go and check it out," said Carl. "What is that in the middle there?" asked Carl. "It almost looks like the shape of a man," said John. "Try to trace it, you always keep a pencil and a pad of paper, don't you?" asked John. "I do have paper, maybe I will trace it before I get out of here," said Carl. "Ok boss," laughed Carl.

CHAPTER TWENTY-ONE

COFFEE TIME

"I'm glad the other guys changed their minds," said Wayne. "They are lucky or we would have to get rid of some loose ends," laughed Matt. "You have to stop watching television, it will destroy your creative mind," said Wayne. "Now you are starting to sound like Mom. Let's get some coffee and fly down Route 68 like we did with our brother's 1979 Pontiac Trans Am. Burt has nothing on us," said Matt. "l remember we passed Haj in his tank like he was still," said Wayne. "Coffee you say, then we are on it. It is officially coffee time," said Wayne.

"We will fuel our car, buy ice coffees, and meet the other guys over there. We are out of here," said Wayne. They were cruising down Route 68 when Wayne caught a glimpse of a black car coming up on them at great speed. He noticed them in his rear-view mirror. "l think we have our buddies right behind us," said Wayne. "Yeah, and they are coming up fast," said Matt. "We will let them get right behind us and then we will smoke the tires," said Wayne. The Pontiac GTO came up on the Chevelle's rear and Wayne looked back and saw Mark and Sam waving. The GTO tapped the rear of the Chevelle. Wayne looked at Matt. "Let's smoke them dude," said Matt. Wayne flipped the Hurst shifter into fourth gear and waved his hand out of the window.

He left them in the dust. "Judge this!" said Wayne. "l just saw some shingles fly off that flea market back there," said Matt. "Pure speed dude, pure speed," said Wayne. "l think I see them coming out of the dust cloud back there," said Matt. "l think we will take it easy on them the center of the Hubbardston is coming up," said Wayne.

They took a right in the center heading towards the Quabbin. As they arrived at the lake, they headed towards the rock-climbing parking lot. They pulled onto a dirt road in an effort to hide their cars. They exited the vehicles and seized their backpacks and climbing gear. They chose a path that headed up towards the rocks. "Hey guys, how did that dust taste back there?" asked Matt. "It was a bit dry for my taste," said Sam. They all laughed about it. "I think this is it guys," said Wayne. They were all looking straight up to the top of the rocks. "We are probably looking at least thirty to forty minutes to climb," said Wayne. "Piece of cake, we have this," said Mark. '"We have to find the right spot and I think that the small statue has something to do with where we are supposed to climb," said Matt.

"If we look around at the base of the rocks, we might find a clue," said Wayne.

They separated and began looking up and down the rocks for a clue. "You might have to look really hard at the rocks. The clue could have faded over the centuries," said Wayne. "Thanks for the heads-up Sherlock," said Sam. Matt stopped in his tracks when he saw engraving in the rocks. He cleared some of the debris with his hands. "Well, I can't believe, it is the same engraving as the statue. Hey guys, I found it over here," yelled Matt. They came running over to Matt. "You get a gold star for today," said Wayne.

Wayne rubbed the engraving and noticed it was a little bit different than the statue. It had the right arm and hand pointing upward. "This is really radical!" said Sam. "Okay enough with the surfing lingo, we have to start climbing," said Wayne.

They unpacked their climbing gear. "Matt and I will climb first and we will secure the ropes so you two can follow," said Wayne. They were about half way securing the ropes, and looking down, taking in the scenery when Wayne said, "We have another fifty feet to go." When Matt grabbed onto a small ledge, it gave out and he fell a few feet until he could grab onto another ledge. "Wow, are you alright over there?" asked Wayne. "It was awesome. I felt a little adrenaline rush for a second. Thank God my climbing skills are still in place," said Matt.

"We are almost at the top. It is just a few more feet," said Wayne. They pulled themselves up the rest of the way. "We made it, now to secure the ropes around these large trees," said Wayne, Matt waved his hands to the other guys. "It is all set, come on up," said Wayne. They sat down on some nearby rocks and waited for the other two.

"Now that we are all here, let's check this place out. It looks like some ruins over here," said Matt. "It looks like it might have been a shrine of some kind," said Matt. "It was probably beautiful back in the day," said Mark. "A bunch of rocks on top of one another and many were knocked over," said Sam.

"l have seen several sticks made into crosses lying around every-where," said Sam. "It probably was used as a burial ground at one time," said Wayne. "Let's follow the stone walk way. It looks like it heads up towards the peak," said Matt. "Be extra careful up this way. There are a lot of loose rocks," said Matt. They hiked up to the peak and looked at the view. New England has the best scenery in the world," said Mark. "Let's not forget the best seafood in the world," said Wayne. "Unless we are missing something, I think we struck out," said Sam. "Maybe we missed something coming up the path," said Mark.

"l really don't see anything up here except the stone walk way. It could have been vandalized not unlike the shrine," said Matt. 't l bet you it is lying down on the ground in pieces somewhere," said Sam. "Guys, we still don't know what we are looking for," said Wayne. "All we have to go by is that little statue," said Matt. '{Nothing I see resem-bles the little man," said Mark. "I see a pumpkin head, but no statue," laughed Matt. They stared straight at the stone walk way. Wayne moved a few feet."Hey, right there. You were standing on it the whole time," said Mark. They knelt down in awe. '"All of this time my big foot was on it," said Wayne. "What do we do now?" asked Sam. "l think that we are supposed to place the little statue here," said Wayne. "What if something terrible happens?" asked Sam. "Well we either find the treasure or another clue," said Wayne.

CHAPTER TWENTY-TWO

LUCKY SEVEN

"Are we all together on this?" asked Wayne. They were all in agreement. Wayne slowly placed the statue on the rock. It made a clicking noise and began to spiral downward towards the rock. 'So much for holding on to the gold statue," said Mark.

They began to hear a rumbling noise. "l knew it! I knew it!" said Sam. The ground began to shake. "Now is our chance to get out of here!" yelled Sam. "Look over there. It appears as if something is coming out of the ground," said Matt.

A large statue resembling the small one began to surface from the ground. Its right arm extended straight out and holding a large bell. "That was wicked cool," said Sam. They cautiously approached the statue. "It is kind of ugly," said Mark. "l don't think that pertains to our next clue," said Matt. They surrounded the huge statue in amazement. "It must stand about eight feet tall all made from stone," said Wayne. "Look, it could even pass for the liberty bell," said Matt. "The guy has pythons for arms," said Wayne.

"I think our next clue must have something to do with the bell," said Matt. "Good observation, my dear Watson, but what?" asked Mark. "I think one of us should take the rope with the stone ball on it and strike it on the side," said Matt. "Good thinking Matt, you thought of it, you do it," said Sam. He proceeded to seize the rope and swing it to hit the inside of the bell. Everyone blocked their ears from the emphatic sound. "l think my ears are ringing," said Wayne. "Yeah, that sound could awaken the dead," said Mark. "It sounds like the ground cracking beneath our feet," said Wayne. "That's not good because we are up on a cliff," said Mark. "I think if we don't get the right number of chimes, we are all going to be gone," said Matt. "Just when I thought this treasure hunt was going smoothly," said Sam.

"I think the closer we get to the treasure the more dangerous it will become," said Wayne. "This wasn't on my application," said Matt.

"Let's look around the statue, maybe it will give us the right number of chimes," said Wayne. "Look up at the eyes. They seem kind of odd," said Mark. "The right eye is very dark and the left eye looks like glass," said Mark. "I think we better find it quickly because I still hear the ground cracking beneath us," said Matt. "The less we move, the better chance we have of not ending up like the coyote," said Wayne.

They stood still examining the statue. "I didn't even think to look at his hands. People usually have five fingers, but this dude has seven fingers on his left hand," said Matt. "That's it! That has got to be it!" said Wayne. "Well, we haven't any time to waste, you know, the coyote," said Sam. "Brilliant, let's try it out," said Sam.

Matt grasped on to the rope a second time. They began to pray for themselves and Matt. Matt started ringing the bell back and forth. The chimes rang out loud, echoing over the valley. Matt held the rope steading waiting for something to occur.

Suddenly, a bolt of light shot down from the sky. It pierced a hole through the forehead and shot out of its left eye. "This is amazing guys. Look the light is pointing down in the valley," said Wayne. They went to the edge of the cliff. I can't believe it. This is beyond anything I could have ever imagined," said Mark. "Look down there the number seven shines on the rock by the waterfall," said Matt. "That's a long way out from here and I don't see any roads out to the waterfall," said Wayne. "Sam are you alright?" asked Mark. "Yeah, I'm just taking it all in," said Sam.

The light vanished not to be seen again. "Well, we had better move on if we are going to make it home before dark," said Wayne. They heard another cracking noise beneath their feet. "I think it is time to go guys," said Matt. "Escape plan!" yelled Wayne. They ran down the stone walk way to the ropes. "Let's get out of here," said Mark. They slid down the ropes to the ground. "Don't you think we should take the ropes?" asked Mark. "Leave it, if we need to, we can use yours and Sam's climbing gear. I don't think we have time anyway. I just heard a car pull up," said Wayne. "Hurry up before anyone sees us," said Matt. They ran into the woods and headed towards the waterfall.

CHAPTER TWENTY-THREE

WE HAVE COMPANY

"Well, here we are man," said John. "Can you remind me what we are doing here?" asked Carl. "We are on a quest for a hidden treasure man," said John. "I think it is all baloney," said Carl. "Come on Mr. Positive. Let's check it out anyway," said John. "Okay, boss," said Carlo They followed the path towards the rocks. John looked behind him, but didn't see Carl. "Hey, come on slow poke while we are still young," said John. "I'm coming. I'm coming, don't rush me," said Carl. John saw Carl turn the corner where they met facing the rocks. "Okay, we are here, can we go home now?" asked Carl.

"Will you get in gear and follow me?" asked John. "Okay boss," said Carl. They followed the rock wall when they came upon two ropes. "Here we go and look it is the same little guy you traced," said Carl.

"Now that just can't be a coincidence," said John. They both looked straight up towards the ropes.

"Who is going to climb up there?" asked Carl. Carl held his stomach with both hands and wiggled it. "Really man, really my wife is a great cook, what can I say?" said Carl. "Alright, you stay here and I'll climb up there," said John. "Don't fall, I really have a weak stomach," laughed Carl.

"Carl, there is one thing that you don't know about me. I'm like spider man when it comes to climbing walls," said John. "Talk is cheap. Let's see spider man climb," laughed Carl. "Alright, I'll show you my skills Carl. Just watch and learn," said John. "I'm watching, but I don't see any action," said Carl. "I'm doing my breathing exercises before I start," said John. "That's good, breathe in and breathe out," said Carl. "I'm ready now. I'll show you how to climb," said John.

John seized the rope and began to climb. "And he's off and climbing," laughed Carl. "I'll grab some shade over here and wait for you," said Carl. "It's all you man. It's all you," said Carl. "The way you climb, we will be here until next week," laughed Carl. "Keep laughing, I don't see you climbing," said

John. Carl held his stomach once more. "Ok enough with the jokes, I appreciate your effort," said Carl.

John was about three quarters the way up when he took a breather. "You are doing great!" yelled Carl. "Oh no John, the rope is unraveling above you!" screamed Carl. John's heart raced as he looked upwards. I don't see anything wrong," said John. "April fools, I got you!" laughed Carl. "Kind of late for April fools don't you think Carl?" asked John. John began climbing once again, making it up to the top. "I made it Carl, so put that in your pipe and smoke it," said John. Carl applauded his determination and grit.

John continued to walk around looking for anything peculiar. He walked up towards the cliff. John's jaw dropped when he came face to face with the large statue. I guess you grew more since the last time I saw you, he said to himself. John climbed to the edge of the cliff. I see a waterfall, and do my eyes deceive, or do I see a group of teenagers headed down that way, John thought.

At that moment, John heard a loud cracking sound. The cliff began to break. He ran as fast as he could before the cliff began to spiral downward. John jumped at the last second onto solid ground as the statue plummeted into the earth. It felt like an earthquake. He thought that it was a close call. He remained on the ground until his heart beat was normal. He turned over looking towards the sky and said "Thank you God for saving me."

John slowly stood up and made his way down to the ropes. John descended down the rope trying to comprehend what just happened. He scanned the ground looking for Carl. "Where are you man?" asked Carl. Carl came from behind a very large tree. "What are you doing there?" asked John. "I saw the whole cliff fall and rocks flying and I had to take cover. I thought that you went down with it," said Carl.

"I really came very close, but I jumped at the last second," said John. "Thank God that he is watching over me man," said John. "Yes, thank God now what did you find up there," asked Carl.

"Well, our little friend which you traced grew up to be a large statue," said John. "Well, did he tell you where the treasure was located?" asked Carl. "Don't be silly. Statues don't speak," said John. "I mean literally," said John. "Alright," said Carl. The statue was looking at a waterfall out to the northern hemisphere. The two cars which you noticed on the way inside had four or five teenagers headed the same way. It can't be a coincidence," said John. "They outnumber us. If we want to catch up to them, we had better get moving," said John.

CHAPTER TWENTY-FOUR

FOLLOW ME

"God that really sounded like an earthquake," said Sam. "I don't know about you guys, but that car we heard makes me think that someone is hot on our trail," said Matt. "Don't be ridiculous. We didn't leave anything behind for someone to be following us," said Mark. "I wouldn't be so sure. They found the cave at the mountain and who knows what else," said Matt.

"Less talk and more walk guys. The quicker we arrive, the harder it will be for anyone to follow us. If they want a piece of me, they will have to go through Sam first," said Matt. "Don't get me involved because I'm an innocent bystander," said Sam. "You dudes are worrying too much and you are not concentrating on what is at hand here," said Wayne. "Well, I like to keep my hands," said Mark. "Are we there yet?" asked Sam. "If we must take action then by all means bring it on!" yelled Matt.

"Come on guys, follow me and hurry," said Wayne. They walked a little quicker through the woods while fighting with the branches, bushes and an infinite number of vines. "Look guys, blueberry bushes, but we don't have time to pick the berries," said Wayne. They walked by the bushes and seized a handful of berries. "You know they are full of antioxidants," said Mark. "What now, we have a nutritionist in the group," said Wayne. "I'm only a teenager and I'll worry about nutrition when I'm one hundred years old," said Matt. "Yeah, really give me a pizza or a juicy burger any day," said Wayne.

"It's on me!" yelled Sam. Sam began brushing off his clothes with his hands. "What is wrong with you now?" asked Matt. "I just walked into a spider web and it was gargantuan. I thought that he was going to carry me away," said Sam. "You are alright. I don't see any spiders on you," said Matt.

"You probably scared it away," said Matt. "I told you your mug scares people and now spiders, so why don't you change it?" asked Wayne. "I'd like to see how you react when you have a gargantuan spider in your face," said Sam. "Spiders are good protein," said Wayne. "Gross! There we go with the health food again," laughed Matt.

"I wish one of us brought a machete or even a chain saw which would help us with all of the vines," said Wayne. "That's what is slowing us down," said Wayne. "It seems like it is taking forever to get to this waterfall," said Mark. Sam looked back to see if anyone was following. "Don't worry Sam because everything is under control," said Wayne. "I just love those apple jacks!" said Wayne.

"Guys, I hear something. Silence!" said Mark. They stood still for a moment. "That is it. It is the waterfall," said Mark. "We must be getting closer," said Sam. "Good observation, my dear Watson. Thank God that we are almost out of the woods. I can't wait for a breath of fresh air," said Matt.

They came upon a hill and slid down to the waterfall. "It is a thing of beauty," said Mark. "Let's not become sentimental," said Wayne. "Well look how massive it is," said Mark. "I think that he is revisiting his sensitive side," said Matt. Wayne pointed up to the rocks. "Up there, that was the rock the hologram appeared on. It was a number seven," said Wayne.

"Except, I really don't see anything up there," said Matt. "Maybe we will have to blast," said Mark. "I really don't think it was the rock, but what really stands out here is the waterfall," said Sam. "Genius," said Wayne. "Let's see if he is right," said Matt. "Let's go explore around the waterfall," said Mark. "There is a slight crack between these rocks. It will be a tight fit, but I think it might lead us behind the waterfall," said Sam.

"You found it, so you should go first Sam," said Wayne. All of the boys attempted to squeeze between the two rocks. "When you said it was a tight fit, you weren't kidding," said Matt. "Luckily, I didn't order

that second large pizza last night," said Mark. They made a little progress. 'I l hope that we don't get stuck in here," said Matt. "Slow down
back there because there is someone stepping on my foot," said Wayne.
"I'm sorry guy, I forgot that you have big feet," said Mark. "Hey, guys, I
think I'm really stuck," said Sam.

"It's probably due to the fact that you have a large head, can anyone pour some grease on it and slide him out?" asked Mark. "l see an
opening ahead only a few more feet," said Sam. "Thank God. I was
becoming a little claustrophobic in there," said Matt. "Wow, it is a little
larger opening than I thought," said Sam. "Very spacious I must say,
my dear Watson," said Mark. "We get the master blaster box and crank
some tunes in here," said Matt.

"Once again there is nothing here representing a seven or anything
for that matter," said Mark.

"Hold on Mark," said Wayne. "Over here guys by the waterfall,"
said Wayne. They gathered around Wayne looking straight down at
his foot. "There we go guys, a number seven," said Wayne. "l see the
seven. I saw the seven, but what are we going to do with the seven?"
asked Mark. "Very, very interesting, except, I don't have a clue," said
Wayne. "Well, we could hammer it out and display it on the wall Mark,"
laughed Matt.

CHAPTER TWENTY-FIVE

THE UNDERGROUND

Wayne knelt down. "We could try turning it, maybe that will do something," said Wayne. Wayne attempted turning it to the left and then to the right. "Nothing happened there. Maybe if you push down on that baby," said Mark. Wayne took both hands and pushed down on it. "Well that really is strike two. I think if I stand and give it a good stomping, maybe, that will do something," said Wayne. He lifted his right leg up high and with all of his force released it and the seven was quickly forced into the rock. "I don't think anything happened. I think you broke it," said Sam.

"I feel something moving under us," said Wayne. "It feels like a tremor because everything is shaking," said Matt. "Look, there are large air bubbles emerged from the water. I told you from the beginning this wasn't a good idea Mark," said Matt. "Hold on! I think the tremor is slowing down," said Matt. "There it stopped and we are still in one piece," said Wayne. "I think that was some scary stuff right there," said Sam.

"I hate to burst your bubble, but whatever we are looking for is underneath us," said Mark. "I really didn't want to get my clothes wet, but guys, it is time to go swimming," said Wayne. "I didn't bring my bathing cap," said Matt. "Well I think it is going to be a new experience for all of us," said Wayne.

"Sam you will have to go back and stand guard," said Wayne. "You are going to leave me down here all alone," said Sam. "Go find a place to hide until we return," said Wayne. Sam went back through the crevice.

"Are you ready for an experience that you will never forget?" asked Wayne. The boys dove into the water plunging deeper when Wayne saw an opening underneath. They swam through the opening plummeting several feet. When they saw a clearing above, they slowly swam into the large opening. They crawled up to the solid ground. They looked around in the underground cave.

"This is so magnificent! Look at all the stalactites and stalagmites," said Mark. "I have to admit of all the places we have been on this treasure hunt, this has to be the most spectacular one of all," said Wayne.

"I see some more of our earlier settler friends laying around," said Matt. "Look one of them is holding a key. It looks like one of those dungeon keys," said Wayne. "I hope this isn't the dungeon," said Mark. "I'll hold on to it. It might come in handy," said Wayne. "I looked the guys over, but nothing to help us out," said Matt. "Guys! Look over here behind this large stalagmite," said Mark. "I found more stairs going upward," said Mark. "Enough with these stairs. You know what happened last time," said Matt.

"Well, I'm checking it out before the trail gets cold," said Wayne. "Well ladies before gentleman," said Mark. "Gentlemen, where?" asked Wayne. They carefully went around the stalagmite and ascended the stairs.

"These walls are very clammy, even these stairs are shorter than usual," said Mark. {"Mark, someday you will make a good wife," laughed Matt. "I hear the waterfall again. We must be reaching the top of it. Hold it guys we are at the end of the stairs. Now it looks like we have to climb up a fifteenth century ladder," said Mark. "I'll go first because it might be unsafe for all of us on it at once," said Wayne.

"Good thinking. We will wait for your signal," said Matt. "What is the signal?" asked Mark. "No one told me about any signals," said Mark. "What is it?" asked Mark. "Right now, you don't want to know," said Wayne. Wayne climbed the ladder. "I think I came upon some sort of trap door," said Wayne.

"I'll try to push on it," said Wayne. Wayne pushed with all of his might, but the door wouldn't budge. "I think something is holding it back. "Give me some light up here," said Wayne. They shined their lights at Wayne. "Oh, there lies the problem. It has a huge padlock which holds a large key. I think that I have the solution," said Wayne.

Wayne pulled the key from his backpack, sliding the key in the hole. Wayne turned the key. "It is being a little stubborn with all of the rust on it, but I'll make it work," said Wayne. Wayne turned the key with a firm grip on it when he heard a click.

"Heads up down there. Here comes the padlock," said Wayne. Wayne pushed up once more on the trap door. "She is budging, but she is one heavy door," said Wayne. Wayne cracked it enough where he could see daylight. "Almost there," said Wayne. Wayne gave it one more shove literally flinging the door over his shoulder. He climbed out above the waterfall. "Come on guys," said Wayne. "Is it safe?" asked Matt. "It is safe now come on up!" said Wayne. They came out of the hole stretching. "There is nothing like fresh air guys and look up there are a bunch of Canadian geese," said Mark.

They went to the edge and looked down. "Hey where is your courageous brother?" asked Matt. The boys yelled for Sam. "Here he comes out from behind that tree. There is the guy with nerves of steel," said Wayne. "Looks like we woke up the dude," said Matt. "Up here Sam!" yelled Wayne. They waved to Sam and he waved back. "Are you holding the fort down there?" asked Mark. He gave them the thumbs up. "We will be down shortly!" yelled Wayne.

"This next clue we are looking for has to be right in front of us," said Wayne. "I have a feeling that the clue was in that underwater cave below us," said Mark. "What is up with the stairs?" asked Matt. "The stairs were probably another exit out of there," said Mark. "We looked all around down there and came up with keys to get us out here for the next clue," said Wayne,

"Well, where is the next clue?" asked Mark. "It has to be around, be patient, like myself and then you will find it. I'll be over here on the rock taking in nature. I guess he doesn't believe in the scientific method," said Wayne. "She blinded me with science," said Matt. "I rest my case," said Wayne.

"I think the guy is right. We have been searching for one hour and came up with nothing," said Matt. "What do you want me to do go over to the dude and tell him that he was right?" asked Wayne. "Ok, I will do it, but I won't like it!" said Wayne. "Hey Mark, I think that you might be right that the clue is below us," said Wayne. "We will head down the ladder and look around," said Wayne. "Sounds like a plan," said Mark. "I don't want to hear any remarks like I told you so," said Wayne. "I don't have to because you took the words right out of my mouth," said Mark. "At least I see you still have a sense of humor," said Wayne.

CHAPTER TWENTY-SIX

PLAN A OR B

Mark went down the ladder and then Matt followed suit. Wayne couldn't believe he was wrong about this one. He took a few steps down when his eyes popped out of his skull. "Wait a minute, I think you guys want to come back up here. I think that I found what we've been looking for," said Wayne. "Up down, up down, is this guy ever going to make up his mind?" asked Mark. They came up from the ladder standing by Wayne. "This had better be good," said Matt. This is more than good, it is great!" said Wayne.

"Just take a look at the rock in the middle of the falls on the edge," said Wayne. "When you said great, I had my doubts, but this is so cool," said Mark. "I told you he was a genius," said Matt.

They intently studied the rock and on it was an embedded number seven. "It's hard to tell us about the next clue," said Wayne. "One question, how are we going to get out there without going over the falls?" asked Matt. "I've been scoping out the area since we arrived here and I saw a fallen tree laying across the river about one hundred yards," said Wayne. Wayne put his hand on Matt's shoulder. "You will cross the tree to the other side. We will throw one of the ends to the rope over to you and tie both ends to the trees closest to the rock," said Wayne. He cringed, "I'll go out there on the rope and very carefully make my way to the rock and see if I can get that thing out," said Wayne.

"There has to be another way because that sounds too dangerous," said Mark. "I'll give you two a minute to come up with a better plan," said Wayne. "Well, it has been one minute have you come up with anything?" asked Wayne. "I have nothing," said Matt. "We'll try it my way and if something goes wrong, I will abort the mission," said Wayne.

Matt wandered up the stream until he came upon the tree Wayne was talking about. "Well here goes nothing," said Matt. Matt sprawled across the tree and inched his way over to the other side.

"Phew, talk about blood pressure. Oh yeah, the guys," said Wayne. Matt headed back towards the falls.

"Hey guys I made it across!" yelled Matt. "What took you so long?" asked Mark. "We were going to have a picnic," said Wayne. "Very funny, do you think it is easy, a lot of skill went into it," said Matt.

"Get ready I'm going to toss you the other end of the rope and you had better catch it," said Wayne.

Wayne winded up and threw the rope as far as he could. The rope landed in the water, but Matt was quick enough to catch the end of it before it went over the falls. "Hey that was a close one," said Matt. "Ok tie the ends around the trees very tight," said Wayne.

They looked across at one another. "You really want to do this because you might plummet to your death," said Mark. "Hey bro, do I get your car if anything happens to you?" asked Matt. "Is this really worth the treasure?" asked Mark. "We can stop here and just forget about all of this and leave it behind," said Mark. "I like that you are sentimental, but I have to do this. We have to do this," said Wayne.

"But if something really goes wrong, promise me, that you guys will find the treasure for me," said Wayne. "Nothing is going to happen now. Let's do it," said Mark.

Everyone gave the thumbs up. Wayne gripped the rope tightly. The powerful current of the river rushed against his legs. The wet rope and the slimy rocks made the journey difficult. "Hang on, your about halfway there," said Matt. "Who thought of this crazy idea anyway?" asked Wayne. "This was all your idea," said Mark. "Next time I have a crazy idea slap me in the face," said Wayne. Wayne saw that he was getting closer to the rock. "I see the seven more clearly. It has two sticks glued together," said Wayne. "If you had listened to my plan in the first place," said Mark. "Yeah, really, you made me cross that unstable tree for nothing," said Matt.

Wayne started laughing. "I'm just kidding guys," laughed Wayne. "I think we have a jokester on our rope," said Matt. "I think we should cut the rope and let him go," said Mark. "Now that is really not funny guys," said Wayne. "Well, get on with it or I might do something drastic over here," said Mark. Wayne made it over to the rock. He was sweating profusely saying, "Everything is under control, nothing to see here, keep on moving."

Wayne climbed onto the rock losing his grip once or twice. He was comfortable enough to grip the number seven in his hands. Wayne pulled upward on it, but it didn't budge. "Oh you are going to be stubborn. Well I can fix that. I'll just have to do some excavation on you," said Wayne. Wayne pulled out his hammer from the backpack.

"Hey guy is that your sister's hammer or did you get that at Toys 'R' Us?" asked Mark. "For your information, I got this one out of your toy box," said Wayne. "Good one," said Matt. "Plus it is lighter than carrying around my two ton hammer all day," said Wayne. "Let me continue using my delicate procedure," said Wayne.

Wayne hammered around the base of the seven loosening up some of the rock and brushing it away. "I used to be an archeologist from way back," said Wayne. Wayne seized the seven and continued hammering around it. "I feel it moving around, but it's not coming out," said Wayne. "Try turning it around and then pulling on it," said Matt.

Wayne did as he was instructed and turned it. When he heard a clicking sound Wayne pulled up on it. It finally released itself from the rock. "I got it!" yelled Wayne. He put it in his backpack. "The rock is cracking from beneath you," yelled Matt. "I thought I was getting a bad vibe," said Wayne. "Hurry, the rock is going over! Hang onto the rope!" yelled Mark. Wayne quickly seized the rope with his right hand. When the rock went over the falls Wayne went to grab the rope with his left hand. "I'm losing my grip," yelled Wayne.

Wayne lost his grip. "Cannonball!" yelled Wayne. This was Wayne's last word as he went over the falls. "No!" the boys screamed. Sam put his hands over his eyes. Mark and Matt looked over the edge, but saw no sign of Wayne.

CHAPTER TWENTY-SEVEN

THE SEARCH

They couldn't believe he hadn't surfaced. "Let's get down there and look for my brother," said Matt. They met with Sam by the river and continued searching for Wayne. "I don't see him," said Sam. "We have to keep searching, he might need our help," said Matt.

They screamed Wayne's name several times, in a state of panic, but never received any response. "I'm getting scared guys. My parents are going to kill me," said Matt. "We'll find him if it takes all day and night," said Mark. "Thanks guys, you are the best friends anyone could ever ask for," said Matt.

"What is that across the river?" asked Sam. "It's just a wild animal," said Mark. "What if the wild animal gets to him and you know," said Matt. "No wild animal swallowed him. We have to think positive here. We have to believe that your brother is still alive and probably ended up down by the river somewhere," said Mark. "Yeah, he is probably headed back this way," said Sam. "Yeah, but I think he would have responded when we yelled out his name," said Matt. "Don't get discouraged guy. Wayne usually takes care of himself pretty well," said Mark. "Yeah, you are right we will just have to keep searching for him," said Matt. "That is the spirit. He is probably down the river having a cold root beer and tacos," said Mark. They laughed in unison for a brief moment and continued with the search. "Hey guys, isn't that his blue shirt he was wearing," said Sam. Matt knelt down by the river bank and reached for the shirt. He seized and held onto it with both fists. Matt smelled the shirt searching for his brother's scent. "Oh yeah, that is his shirt. I can smell his body odor," said Matt. "Are you crying?" asked Sam. "No it is just the odor that is tearing my eyes," said Matt. "I just remembered that I borrowed ten dollars from him. I was going to pay him back, I swear," said Matt.

A hand squeezed Mark's shoulder. "Is that you Wayne?" asked Mark. "It had better be you," said Mark. They looked up and saw a man holding onto Mark. They backed away from the man. "Who are you and what do you want?" asked Matt. "My name is not important here, but you kids know what we want," said John. "I resent that remark. Who is the person with you?" asked Mark. John looked back and couldn't see Carl. "If you have to know we swim here all the time," said Matt. "I don't see you wearing any swim trunks," said John. "We are kind of shy," said Sam.

Carl slowly approached them breathing heavily. "Where have you been man?" asked John. "I didn't know we were going to hike through the jungle for miles. I had to rest a couple of times just to catch my breath. My body isn't made to travel long distances," said Carl. "Enough, if you kids don't tell us where the treasure is right now, we will duct tape you to the trees and leave you there," said John.

"What are you a tough guy?" asked Matt. "I'll show you how tough I am," said John. "Treasure, treasure, treasure, we really don't know what you are talking about," said Mark. "I think you are in the wrong country if you are looking for treasure," said Matt.

"We found the rock you tipped over with the map of the Quabbin on the island. Also, we think you kids had something to do with the opening of the cave at the mountain. I've been up and down that mountain and have never seen a cave," said John. "I guess you didn't look hard enough Sherlock," laughed Matt, "That proves my point, you have been in that cave and probably found something that led you here," said John. "I think he's been smoking something," laughed Matt. "I guess it is time to take drastic measures here," said John.

"Run! Run! Run!" yelled Wayne. Wayne came out from behind a large tree. "Run guys!" said Wayne. Wayne ran and slid under John's legs sending him flying into the river. They ran back into the woods towards the cars. "Did you see that?" asked Wayne. "It was my ninja skills," said Wayne. They continued to run for about ten minutes through the woods.

"Slow down, I think we lost them," said Wayne. "Where have you been? We thought that you were gone," said Matt. "We searched for you over one hour and you were behind that tree all of this time," said Mark. "No, but I did end up downstream a bit. I hid because I knew we were going to have company," said Wayne. "How did you know about them?" asked Sam. "Instinct, my ninja instincts my dear Watson," said Wayne. "Plus, I saw them through the woods coming this way as I almost plummeted to my death," said Wayne. "Anyway, we are all safe now, and we should get to our cars before sunset," said Wayne.

They made it to their cars. "We will meet you at your house Mark in the morning to figure out this artifact," said Wayne. "Dude, you can give me the ten dollars once this is all over," laughed Wayne. "You didn't go down the stream, you probably hid behind the tree listening to every word," said Matt. "You will never know that will be my little secret," said Wayne. They headed for home.

CHAPTER TWENTY-EIGHT

BREAKFAST AT THE ESTATE

Wayne and Matt found their parents in the living room watching television. "I see you boys made it home on time," said Dad. "What happened to your shirt?" asked Dad. "It's the new style, you know styling and profiling. A male model has nothing on me," laughed Wayne.

"Where are the other two?" asked Dad. "They went home. We have to get up early and meet them at their house," said Wayne. "You are not still looking for that treasure when I told you not to," said Dad.

"No we got bored of looking. There's no action in hunting for treasure," said Matt.

"Well you boys better go up to bed if you need to get up early," said Dad. "Your right Dad. Goodnight Mom. Goodnight Dad," said the boys. The boys remained together talking. "I know every time we get one step closer to the treasure. It's really becoming very dangerous. In addition, we now have two men after us," said Matt. "I think if we can keep a cool head and avoid any trouble, we will get through this," said Wayne. "We will have to be cautious with every step we take," said Wayne. "All I know is that it was a close one today with you going over the falls. We thought we lost you and then those guys just showing up. They know something about the treasure and I don't think they will be giving up any time soon," said Matt. "I wouldn't worry about them. We left them in the dust," said Wayne. "I think we should get our sleep because we will need it tomorrow," said Wayne.

"Goodnight dude. Yeah, goodnight John Boy lights out," said Wayne.

Wayne awakened to the smell of bacon, eggs, toast and coffee brewing downstairs in the kitchen. Breakfast being the most important meal of the day, he decided to make his way there. First, he checked to see if Matt was still asleep, but noticed that his bed was already made. He thought that Matt was already downstairs kissing up to his parents. Wayne chose to infiltrate the system and prevent Matt from becoming their favorite. "I can't let this happen," said Wayne.

"Good morning Mom. It smells really great throughout the house," said Wayne. "Good morning son.

What was all of the yelling upstairs?" asked Mom. "I had the volume of the television too loud," said Wayne. Wayne looked through the cupboards. "No hash, Mom," said Wayne. "Do I have to remind you boys all of the time?" asked Mom. Wayne mumbled. "I'm not running a restaurant here," said Mom. "Go sit down until breakfast is ready!" said Mom. "Ok I'll just pour myself a cup of coffee," said Wayne.

"I'll go visit Dad in the living room," said Wayne. "Hey Captain, how is the estate running today?" asked Wayne. "It is running like a top. I'm just lounging today son," said Dad. "What is in the Gardner News today?" asked Wayne. "You know the Gardner News. No news is always good news," said Dad.

Wayne sat down on the couch and Matt in the rocking chair. "Here is something in the news about that cave they found up at the mountain," said Dad. "Wow, they are really milking that project. I thought they would be done with that one week ago," said Matt. "They have to justify their paychecks," said Wayne. "Anyway, they think they found enough evidence up there that the early settlers brought over a substantial amount of gold, except, back then they didn't have much use for it. The skeletal remains show evidence that many people died trying to find it. The historians say that the settlers left clues within this county," said Dad. "What do they have to support this theory?" asked Wayne. "They don't say, probably top secret," said Dad. "I think it is just a theory like you said because they don't have any clue," said Matt.

"I know many people have died hiding the gold. Maybe it is better if no one found the gold," said Dad. "Right on Dad! Give me some skin!" said Wayne. "They did find four sets of footprints. The size of the sneakers makes them suspect teenagers. They say that the teenagers might have found something, but they don't know. They didn't know how to read the hieroglyphics," said Dad.

"The historians are a bunch of geniuses. They think they know it all," said Wayne. "Well, let them keep guessing it is better that way," said Matt. "It will probably be a mystery and that is all it will ever be," said Wayne. "You boys don't have to get defensive," said Dad. "Unless, you are the teenagers with your two friends. You four were always exploring up at the mountain," said Dad. "Ok. We will let you in a little secret. We know the four teenagers that were up there before the hikers stumbled upon it," said Wayne. "Whatever they found up there should be given to the historians," said Dad. "l think they will eventually," said Matt. "l trust you boys will make the right decision," said Dad.

"Come on, time to get it! Breakfast is ready," said Mom. "I'll bring a whole slab of cooked bacon and another gallon of that great coffee," said Wayne. Mom looked at him with a smile. "You will get what you get and like it," said Mom. "Can't you take a joke Mom?" asked Wayne. "Sit down and eat before I give you something to really laugh about," laughed Mom. "Sit down like your brother over there and be quiet," said Mom. "My brother with the halo over his head," said Wayne.

They finished eating breakfast. "That was a great breakfast and you are the best cook in the world Mom," said Wayne. "Put that in your pipe Matt," laughed Wayne. They helped clean up and did the dishes. "Sorry, Mom, but we have to run," said Wayne. "We have to meet up with Mark and Sam at their house," said Matt. "Well you boys stay safe and don't come home too late," said Mom.

CHAPTER TWENTY-NINE
TIME CAPSULE

Wayne turned onto a very steep road called Nutting Street. "Did I ever tell you that our sister and I tried walking up this street to the school? It was in the winter time and I think I was six years old. We couldn't walk up the street because it was sheer ice. We tried walking up it, but we just slid back down. We overcame each obstacle and walked through the neighbor's yard," said Wayne. "Don't quote me on this, but I think once we arrived at the school it was cancelled," said Wayne. "Now that is a story for the record books," said Matt.

They drove up the hill towards Mark's house. "I see Mark is still trying to do tricks on his skateboard," said Wayne. Sam was going over a jump he made for his BMX. Wayne pulled up in front of their drive- way. "Another late night and early morning," said Mark. "Ok guys, now that you have got it out of your system. We have to concentrate on the artifact at hand," said Wayne.

Wayne took it out of his backpack and laid it on the ground.

"If anyone has a hint on what this does feel free to give me your opinions," said Wayne. Matt picked it up and examined it very closely. "What do you see my number two son?" laughed Sam. "I think we are finally stuck and that we have come to the end of searching for this treasure and that is assuming that there really is a treasure," said Matt. "I don't see anything significant on it, not even a clue. Perhaps Mark was right that the clue we were looking for was in that underwater cave," said Matt.

"You mean I risked my neck for nothing?" asked Wayne. "I hate to say it, but we all did the same thing," said Matt. "I didn't think that the adventure would come to an end," said Wayne. "Unless we return to the Quabbin and give it a second look," said Mark. "You guys can if you want, but I think I'm packing it up," said Wayne. "If you are then we are as well because we are all friends and we stick together," said Mark.

"Remember guys, this is where we buried that time capsule," said Wayne. "That brings back memories," said Matt. "Do you even remember what we put in it?" asked Wayne. "I think we put in some baseball cards, stamps and I can't remember the rest. Maybe we should leave clues to the time capsule someday," said Matt. "Maybe in one hundred years someone will find it," said Sam.

"I guess the historians, archeologists and even those bad guys are out of luck," said Wayne. "Yeah, they will be still looking around for the treasure, but they will never find it without the next clue," laughed Matt. "We will be at Hampton Beach playing video games," said Mark. "I think this calls for a road trip guys," said Wayne. "Asteroids, Space Invaders, Galaga are all waiting to be played," said Sam.

"Let's get out of here and get rid of that so-called number seven," said Wayne. Matt whipped it to the ground. Once it stuck in the ground the top broke off and a light shot out quickly. The boys fell to the ground. "What was that noise?" asked Sam. Matt slowly moved towards the artifact. "Careful, Matt because that think is probably able to shoot out more of that light," said Mark.

Matt bent down to pick it up. He retrieved it with his hand and quickly dropped it. "Hey that thing is extremely hot," said Matt. "I'll cool it off," said Sam. Sam poured his soda on it and watched the steam come off of it. "That's great Sam you cooled it off, but now it is sticky," said Matt. "You win some and you lose some," said Sam. Matt peered down the opening. "Hey guys it is hollow and there is nothing in it," said Matt.

"Look guys the top of it is broken. I see something sticking out of it," said Mark. Matt pulled out a piece of paper and opened it. "I can't read this is strange words which I can't decipher," said Matt. Wayne seized it from Matt. "Let me see then. I've taken about one million languages in high school. I think that I'm highly qualified for this prestigious task," said Wayne. "Oh no, I didn't bring my smart glasses," laughed Wayne. "I'll just have to wing it," said Wayne. "Come on! Get on with it," said Mark. Wayne cleared his throat and began to read "With this rod of light and with the light of the full moon it will show you through the marsh to your next destination."

"Guy, the marsh meaning the swamp?" asked Sam. "I don't know about you, but swamps frighten me, especially during the day, but I'm sure they are more horrific at night," said Sam. "Where is the swamp that he is talking about?" asked Mark. "The only swamp we know of is the one between Gardner and Westminster," said Matt.

"The swamp that is on both sides of Route 2A," said Mark. "That one is huge. Well we know we can't split up with only one rod of light," said Wayne. "Even if we choose one side and it takes all night, so be it. If it is the wrong side, we will have to wait for another night with a full moon," said Mark. "Well that is the chance we will have to take," said Wayne. "No one said this adventure would be easy," said Matt.

"The question is when is the next full moon?" asked Mark. "Again being a meteorologist from way back, the next full moon is in three nights," said Wayne. "If it is astonishing and brilliant that you know all of these things," said Sam. "Thank you, I will be here all day," said Wayne. "Except, I think that we are all brilliant," said Wayne. "I'm really starting to love this quest for the gold," said Matt.

"Speaking of love, at the end of the adventure should we find the treasure, I'm going to look inside the church on Sunday," said Wayne. "We are all with you on that one," said Mark. "Then it is a plan," said Wayne.

"Well what are we going to do with ourselves for three days?" asked Matt. "It's like we planned at the beginning go to the arcade up at Hampton Beach and continue to Whalom Park to play miniature golf. In addition, I can show you my ninja skills. I can't show you all of them because many of them are ancient secrets from late ancestors of the past," said Wayne.

"Now that we have our agenda planned there is only one thing which we have forgotten," said Mark. "I think we covered everything," said Wayne. Mark looked over at the house and then they all looked at one another and spoke "Parents." "Dudu that is right because we have a curfew at night," said Wayne. "We could sneak out at night and meet down by the swamp," said Sam. "That's a good idea, but they still might find out," said Matt.

"How are they going to know?" asked Sam. "Some parents know they just do," said Mark. "I have an idea you and Matt can ask your parents to ask our parents to sleep over your house," said Mark. "Genius Mark," said Wayne. "We know that our parents don't call each other. It is definitely a fool proof plan," said Mark.

"Why didn't we think of it before?" asked Matt. "Well, anyway, I'm glad I thought of it," laughed Wayne. "When we go up to Hampton Beach and visit the arcades, I will get a high score on every game against you. Three of you have to quit calling me pumpkin head," said Sam.

"You know that you will have a hard time winning your brother here. The video games are all mine," said Mark. "Ok mad scientist. I think that we are ready to rock and roll," said Wayne. "Let's go pumpkin head," said Matt.

They passed the front door to the house when Mark's mother said "Are you boys playing with firecrackers again?" "No Mom, what gave you that idea?" asked Mark. "I heard a loud bang and saw a very bright light," said Mark's Mom. They looked at one another and Mark shrugged his shoulders. "Stop whatever is causing the light or go to your rooms," said Mark's mother. "Wayne and Matt can go home," said Mark's mother. "We won't do it again," said Mark. His mother went back inside the house. "Guy your mother looked angry," said Matt. "I guess we dodged one there," said Mark. "Well, I'm ready for a little arcade action and some competition," said Mark. "Road trip!" yelled Matt.

CHAPTER THIRTY

THAT WAS FAST

The boys were sitting at the picnic table. "I don't know about you, but these three days have flown by," said Sam. "Yeah, but we did have tons of fun," said Mark. "I can't forget Sam's face when Mark crushed him on Asteroids and Space Invaders," said Wayne. "It looked like the kid next to us when his friend beat him," said Matt. "Yeah, what was the kid's name anyway?" asked Mark. "I think he said his name was Sherman," said Wayne. "Every time Mark beat Sam his jaw would drop lower and lower," laughed Matt. "Yeah, but I beat Mark at Galaga," said Sam. "Sam you know what that means," said Mark. "I've had enough. It's all I've heard on the return trip home," said Sam. "We will spare you this time," said Wayne.

"What about yesterday when we went down that steep hill in the cemetery? We had to see who would come closest to the cliff at the bottom," said Sam. "Well we all know who won," said Wayne. "I think I should have won that one because I came the closest without going over," said Sam. "Yeah, Sam but we have to give it to Matt because he went over and almost died," said Wayne. "When we looked at him down there, we all felt how painful it must have been," said Mark. "How are you feeling today guy?" asked Wayne. "A lot of bumps and bruises, but I'm rugged," said Matt. "Alright, I admit that it was pretty cool when the three of us stopped and Matt kept going. Flying off the cliff, he definitely won hands down!" said Sam.

"I think we should have a dare that whoever goes off the cliff and lands in S. Bents lumberyard wins," said Mark. "That sounds like a plan," said Matt. "First we have to keep our plans for tonight," said Wayne.

"I think we should look over our check list," said Wayne. "The boat is present. Matt and I dropped the boat off behind that abandoned building with the large chair in front using our friend's truck last night," said Wayne. "The ropes, flashlights and flares are present. They have been placed inside the boat," said Matt. "What are the flares for?" asked Sam. "We have them just in case we really become lost and perhaps someone will see it and rescue us," said Mark.

"Why don't we bring a compass?" asked Sam. "It can't be that hard to read," said Sam. "We should bring the one from the Boy Scouts," said Matt. "The sunglasses are necessary," said Wayne. "Why are we bringing the sunglasses?" asked Mark. "After the light brightens the back yard, I think we are really going to need to wear them," said Wayne. "I think we should bring some bug spray as well since the mosquitos are huge in the swamp," said Sam. "Oh, we will bring the bug spray. We don't want the mosquitos to carry us away," said Wayne. "What about the munchies and the soda?" asked Sam. They looked at one another. "(No one thought to bring any munchies or soda?" asked Wayne. "Well you guys had better stop at Smitty's Variety Store on your way home," said Wayne.

"Don't forget our night vision goggles," said Matt. "Last but not least, don't forget the master blaster box because we need good Christian tunes," said Mark. "I think that we have everything on the list," said Wayne. "One more question, is everyone ready for this adventure?" asked Wayne. "If you are then put your hands together," said Wayne. Sam put his hand on top of Mark's and Matt finally put his hand on top of Sam's. "Guy, that is not funny. I'm a delicate flower," said Sam. They chanted one, two three and four.

The following day the neighbors looked over and studied the boys. "Man, you have some curious neighbors," said Mark. "You are telling me. I think that they can't help being curious," said Wayne. "I hate to say it but that black van with the dark tinted windows has been parked near the cemetery for a few hours now," said Sam. "Maybe it is someone visiting a deceased loved one," said Mark.

"I didn't see anyone come out and I didn't see anyone going inside," said Sam. "You think it is our friend from Boston?" asked Wayne. "Yeah, but how did they find out where we live?" asked Matt.

"They have infinite contacts. He probably wrote down our license plate number and got the information from the Registry of Motor Vehicles," said Mark. "They probably have surveillance installed over at your home," said Matt.

"This isn't good because they are watching every move we make," said Mark. "Don't look at either one of them, just pretend that you don't see them," said Sam. "Good idea, but this means a change of plans," said Wayne. "We will have to abort the mission," said Matt. "There is no way we are letting tonight pass with a clear sky and a full moon," said Wayne.

"So, what is the plan?" asked Sam. "We can't take our cars tonight because they will be expecting us. We will have to sneak out our BMX bikes and take a few trails going through our neighbor's yard to ensure that we are not being followed. When we have reached Route 2A we will meet at the boat," said Wayne. "That is the plan?" asked Mark. "You two are closer to Route 2A, so make sure you are not being followed," said Wayne.

"It could be those two bad guys at the waterfalls," said Sam. "It is impossible because we left them in the dust. When his friend was fishing his buddy out of the water, we were already in Gardner," said Matt. "Do you think these guys from Boston know anything about the treasure?" asked Mark. "I think that might have found clues up at the mountain that a treasure might exist. We found the maps at the farm house. In addition, they don't have this particular rod of light and the next destination for the treasure," said Wayne.

"There might be another clue," said Wayne. "What?" asked Sam. "There is another clue? I thought this was the last clue to the treasure," said Sam. "It might be guy, but it didn't really say that the treasure would be there," said Matt. "The only way to find out is by going tonight or trying to travel further," said Wayne. "I think we should buckle up for the ride because it might be rough," said Mark.

"When and if we do find the treasure, what will happen at that point?" asked Sam. "I hate to say it but we tell the guys from Boston that we found the treasure. They estimate how much it is worth and pay us the finder's fee," said Wayne. "After everything we have experienced, and the size of the treasure, I'm sure it will be a very generous finder's fee, so relax," said Wayne.

"What is plan B if plan A fails?" asked Mark. "We stick to plan A so that we will never need plan B," said Wayne. "Anyone up for baseball before tonight's great adventure?" asked Matt. "Yeah, of course. I like hitting the baseball over the one-hundred-foot tree in the woods," said Mark. "Wow, every time we hit that ball into the woods, your dog Belle went in there and always retrieve it," said Sam. "Belle, she is the greatest dog in the world," said Wayne. "Our cat Inky comes in with a few battle scars, but I hate to see what the other cat looks like," said Matt.

"Well, it is getting to be dinner time and we have to go inside to clean up," said Wayne. "What time do we meet at the boat?" asked Mark. "I think a good time would be at ten tonight," said Wayne. "'Don't forget to tell your parents that you are sleeping over and we will do the same. Don't forget the munchies on the way home," said Matt. The GTO smoked the tires down the road and disappeared over the bridge.

CHAPTER THIRTY-ONE

HOME FOR THE NIGHT

Wayne and Matt went into the house. "Something smells good in here, let me guess your infamous hot dogs and beans Mom," said Wayne. "You boys get washed up and tell your friends next time not to smoke the tires down the street because no one likes that smell," said Mom. "Mom it is one of the greatest odors in the world unless you put bleach down first it might burn your eyes a little, but boy what a smoke show!" said Wayne.

"Bleach? Really?" asked Matt. "When I worked down at the gas station on Timpany Boulevard, I always closed up at eleven o'clock. Well, one day, a guy pulled up in his Charger around ten thirty on the street. He came in and told me if I really wanted to see a smoke show, he would pour bleach underneath his back tires and lit them up for about five minutes. It was the greatest smoke show ever, but the odor lingered for a while. He pulled into the gas station and changed his two back tires," said Wayne. "Enough stories, go get cleaned up!" said Mom.

They finished up their dinner and helped Mom clean up. Then they went into the living room and sat down on the couch. Dad was watching the news. "Anything good on tonight Clint Eastwood?" asked Wayne. "I didn't see anything interesting in the television guide," said Dad. "How about on HBO?" asked Matt. "Nothing. It is too bad that they didn't have The Three Stooges station, then we would all laugh," said Wayne.

Wayne whispered to Matt. "I think we buttered up Dad enough, just in case Mom says no. Then we have a good chance Dad will say yes," said Wayne. They went into the kitchen. "Mom we have a question. Mark's parents said they didn't mind if we slept over tonight, so can we?" asked Wayne. "I'm busy go and ask your father," said Mom. "Hey Dad, Mom said to go and ask you if we could sleep over Mark's house?" asked Wayne. "You boys have been out late every night for the last few months. I think you boys should stay in for one night. It won't hurt you to spend some time with your mother and myself," said Dad. Wayne and Matt looked at one another stunned. "Ok then we will go upstairs and call Mark on the phone and tell him that we can't sleep over," said Wayne.

"'Hello Mark, our parents said that we couldn't sleep over due to all of the late nights we have been spending out," said Wayne. "Guy, our parents said yes, so what are we going to do?" asked Mark.

"Don't worry we will think of something. The plan is still on for tonight. We will meet you at the boat as planned," said Wayne. "Sam and I will say a prayer for you two not to get caught," said Mark. "We will see you two guys tonight," said Mark. Wayne hung up the receiver to the phone and looked at Matt.

"There is no way you are involving me in your escape plan this time," said Matt. "We have it all planned out. We can't quit now," said Wayne. "Well, what if we get caught this time? We will be grounded for life!" said Matt. "Why don't we wait for the next full moon?" asked Matt. "We really can't wait because there are others looking like those two guys from Boston and they could be right behind us on our trail and if they figure it out then they will be the first ones to find the treasure," said Wayne.

"They wouldn't be spying on us if they knew where the treasure was located," said Matt. "Good point, but we will just have to take that risk," said Wayne. "Well let's say I'm in just exactly how are we going to escape?" asked Matt. "I figure we will jump out of our bedroom window facing the cemetery," said Wayne. "Do you know how much of a drop that is going to be, it is at least fifteen feet. We will most assuredly break our necks," said Matt. "How about if we sneak downstairs and go out of the door," said Matt. "I thought of that too, but it will make too much noise and we will certainly get caught," said Wayne.

"Anyway, the guys will be waiting for us. We are the backbone of this operation," said Wayne. "Yeah, and we will probably break our back bones jumping," said Matt. "It is almost nine and we don't have much time. Either you jump or stay behind. I'm jumping to meet up with the guys and find the treasure," said Wayne. Matt sat there contemplating for a few minutes. "It's now or never guy, which is it going to be?" asked Wayne. "Ok let's do this, but if I break my neck, I'm coming back to claim your treasure and mine," said Matt.

They opened the window and looked down. "It looks further than I thought," said Wayne. "No way guy, I was the greatest stuntman back in the day," said Wayne. "Give me my backpack and yours and I will throw them down first," said Wayne. Wayne squatted on the window-sill, and saying a quick prayer, then jumped. He landed on his feet and did a quick somersault. "I told you the stuntmen have nothing on me. Now it is your turn," said Wayne. "Don't hesitate because we don't have much time," said Wayne. "Just do it," said Wayne. Matt pushed off and jumped to the ground. He landed on his feet and then fell to his knees. "You alright, you didn't tuck and roll," said Wayne. "I think I'll be ok.

I just landed a little awkward," said Matt. "Can you ride your bike?" asked Wayne. "I'll be fine. I just have to walk it off," said Matt. "I told you a piece of cake. I had no doubt in my mind we could make that jump," said Wayne. "Ok Einstein, what is next?" asked Matt. "I say we take a few hills through the woods and make it over to Mark's house. It is the quickest way to Route 2A," said Wayne. "I see that the van is gone. Maybe they gave up on the search," said Matt. "I wouldn't count them out just yet," said Wayne.

CHAPTER THIRTY-TWO

ROUTE 2A

"We might be a little behind on time, but we can make it up with the short cuts," said Wayne. "Let's ride guy!" said Matt. They jumped on their bikes crossing the street and made their journey through the woods. They came to the top of the hill onto a side street. "No signs of trouble yet, make sure you avoid any headlights," said Wayne. They made it down towards Mark's house through the neighbors' yards. They stopped by Miller's garage out on Route 2A. "We made it this far without any activity on the roads," said Matt. "Here comes a vehicle!" screamed Wayne. They hid behind a car at the garage.

A van passed by very slowly. "Hey I think you spoke too soon," said Wayne.

"Hey that was the van by our house," said Matt. "Hold on! Here comes another one," said Wayne. "I'm sure Gardner and Westminster are crawling with these guys," said Matt. "They are a thorn in our side," said Wayne. "You really are asking me what it means, are you serious? I can't even answer you. You will have to find out on your own," said Wayne. "Anyway, we don't have time for trivia because we have to get to the boat," said Wayne.

"It is approximately one mile to the boat. We don't have many places to hide," said Matt. "We will have to be like the wind and get there without being seen. Are you sure you are really ready for this?" asked Wayne. "Take a few deep breaths and let's go," said Wayne.

They quickly pedaled down Route 2A. "We are going to make it and they will never see us," yelled Wayne. Wayne saw Matt slowing down on his bike. "Come on now catch up we can't slow down now," said Wayne. "I think when I jumped out of the window, I really bumped my knee," said Matt. "I'll catch up to you," said Matt. "That's the spirit. I'll see you at the boat," said Wayne.

Wayne made it to the abandoned building. He went down the dirt driveway behind the building and hid his bike in the woods. Mark and Sam came out of the woods. "Where have you guys been?" asked Mark. "It is a long story. We had to hide down at Miller's garage. Those vans which we saw are prowling up and down Route 2A," said Wayne. "Where is your brother?" asked Mark. "He was right behind me. He is moving a little slower because he banged his knee jumping out of our window," said Wayne.

"You guys jumped out of a window? That was your escape plan?" asked Mark. "You both could have broken your necks," said Mark. "Well, where is he?" asked Sam. "I'm telling you he was right behind me. Look out here comes one of those vans. Hide!" yelled Wayne. The van drove past the building.

"I think that they spotted us because it is turning around," said Sam. "That is really impossible. How could they see us behind the building?" asked Wayne. "Where is your brother?" asked Mark. "Maybe they saw him," said Mark. "Oh no, that is not good. We have to leave because now they are coming down the driveway," said Wayne.

They ran into the woods where they hid behind the boat with their eyes peeled to the van. "They want to find us to learn the exact location of the treasure. I don't believe they actually want to murder us," said Wayne. "Oh, what a relief," said Sam. "Then they can keep the treasure and we won't collect the finder's fee," said Mark.

"One of the dudes is getting out of the van. It's hard to see his face, but it almost looks like Mr.

Stevens," said Wayne. thought I saw one of the kids on a bike from that store Stop and Cop," said Mr. Stevens. "We have been watching their homes all day and have not seen any activity," said Scott. "They could have slipped out when you went to Burger King," said Mr. Stevens. "It is possible," said Scott. "Shine your light over there by the woods," said Mr. Stevens. "Negative, either he hid when he saw us or headed back home," said Scott. "Get back in the van. We will find him, even if we have to send out a chopper tomorrow," said Mr. Stevens. They returned to Route 2A heading back towards Gardner.

"Phew! That was a close call, but we are still missing your brother," said Mark. "Hey! Here he comes down the driveway," said Mark. They exited the woods to meet Matt. "Where have you been? We almost were kidnapped by those guys," said Wayne. "What is that awful odor?" asked Mark. They stepped back a bit when Matt took off his shirt after swimming in the swamp. He had leeches attached to his skin which Wayne removed. "Leeches are a good source of protein," said Wayne.

"What happened?" asked Sam. "What happened? I'm sure my brother filled you in regarding our escape plan. Well once we made a dash from Miller's Garage, I banged my knee and felt more pain from pedaling so fast. I couldn't keep up with my brother. I had to jump over the guard rail with my bike. When I saw the van heading towards me, I found myself up to my neck in the swamp. Then I turned around and headed in your direction," said Matt.

"After it disappeared down the road, I finally pulled myself out of the swamp and made a quick escape to the boat. It was some escape plan," said Matt. "We can use that bug spray and maybe it will get rid of the odor," said Mark. They took out the repellent and sprayed themselves until the can became empty. "That is just great! Now I really will be devoured by the bugs and itching for weeks!" said Sam. "It might not be that bad Sam," said Mark. "When we smell like elderly women, I'm certain everything in the swamp will vacate. I think you are safe," said Mark.

"Well, we ditched our bikes and don't know if we should travel to the right or to the left of Route 2A," said Matt. "Why don't we leave it up to the genius over here?" asked Matt. "That is super genius to you," said Wayne. "You guys are putting a lot of pressure on me. If I get it wrong you might throw me in the swamp," "Don't give us any ideas," said Mark. They looked at him with a stern expression.

"O.K. on a more serious note, everyone would probably take the right side. They would take into consideration the earlier settlers might have thought the same and chosen the left side. Unless they utilized reverse psychology on us. I would have chosen the left side," said Wayne.

"Didn't I tell you guys pure genius," said Matt. "I would have tossed a coin, but we will go with your theory," said Mark. "It is kind of better that way. I didn't want to carry the boat across the road," said Sam. "Is it just a coincidence that we put the boat on the left side?" asked Sam. "Or is it the supernatural?" asked Matt. "Well, I guess we will find out, won't we?" asked Sam.

"Guys, let's get the boat in the water while we still have a bright full moon in the sky," said Wayne. They dropped the boat in the water and loaded it with the backpacks. Wayne took the front seat. Mark and Sam were rowing first in the middle seat. Since he still had a pungent odor on his person, Matt sat in the back seat. "Are you ready for the journey of a lifetime?" asked Wayne. "Before we go, did you guys remember to bring some munchies?" asked Sam. "We took the most nutritional ones we could find rock candy, bottle caps, candy necklaces, cigarette candy, smarties, soda and much more," said Mark. "Let's roll guys," said Matt. "When Pepe La Pew says roll, let's row," laughed Wayne. "We are off to find the treasure!" said Mark.

CHAPTER THIRTY-THREE

SWAMP FEVER

Mark and Sam began rowing now knowing what was in the future. This was a new quest of unchartered territory. Wayne removed the rod of light from his backpack and placed it down near his person. "Lights and shades on because tonight because I think we are in for a wild ride," exclaimed Wayne. "How can that be?" "We are in a row boat," Mark reminded him. "Silence!" yelled Wayne. "In all of my life, the entire sixteen years of it, I would have never thought that I'd be in a boat in the swamp of all places searching for a treasure," said Matt. "I have a funny story about the swamp with our buddy Lance," said Wayne.

"So, what is the story?" asked Sam. "You have heard that expression, if I tell you than I will have to kill you," laughed Wayne. "Don't leave us hanging," said Mark. "It is for another time. Right now, it is onward and upward," said Wayne.

As Mark and Sam rowed the boat deeper into the swamp Sam commented. "'We will look back on how much fun and excitement this was when we're older. "I will never forget you guys," said Sam. "Are you becoming sentimental on us again? Is that a tear I see running down your cheek?" asked Matt. "No that is a tear from your body odor and the swamp," said Sam. "Hey guys, relax. We will all have a group hug later,"

"I don't think we are in Kansas anymore," said Mark. "Do you see anything out of the ordinary?" asked Wayne. "Not yet, but we just scratched the surface," said Matt. "Give me some of those munchies.

I'm on break!" said Wayne. "Wow, a Sky Bar, that is s good score guys. I wonder what the nutritional value is on the back of the bar. There isn't any nutritional value. Excellent," said Wayne.

"The swamp is so desolate, and the trees are dead," said Mark. "You have a beautiful full moon with all of the stars surrounding it. You have the birds, the plant life and the creatures which live in the swamp," said Wayne. "Wow, you should be a poet," said Mark. "Thank you. I will be here all night," said Wayne.

"l don't know about you guys, but I've been craving Applejacks since the waterfall," said Sam. "I wonder why. Maybe it was something in the air," said Matt. "We have been rowing for about one hour. I think you chose the wrong side," said Mark. "Don't be discouraged. We haven't even covered one half of the swamp," said Wayne. "The smell from the swamp is brutal," said Sam. "Keep it up Sam. I'll get up and throw you to the frogs," said Matt.

"l think you might want to wish upon one of those falling stars up there Sam," said Mark. "What for?" asked Sam. "I'm sure the frogs will be happy with one live bait, but they will be more than thrilled with both of you," laughed Matt.

Suddenly, something swooped down and lightly grazed Sam's head. "What was that?" asked Sam. "A loon," said Matt. "I resent that remark," said Sam. "Not you, the bird is called a loon. It probably thought that you were a fish out of the water. It found out when it swooped down that your head was too large to hold," said Matt. "At first, I thought it was one of the pterodactyls that was going to take me away to its nest," said Sam. "I don't think they would like the cuisine," said Matt.

"l think that we should head down to the left. I saw something," said Wayne. "It had better be good because my arms are getting tired," said Sam. "The moonlight shining on the water might have been another clue," said Wayne. "Look over there, I see an eerie glow," said Mark. "There are actually different gases which come from the swamp and cause a glow," said Sam. "Where did you hear that one genius?" asked Matt. "l think it could have been on the history channel or I could have just made it up, but you will never know," said Sam.

"Yeah, that will be the first thing on my bucket list when I go back to school and ask the teacher," laughed Matt. "Slow down guys because we are approaching the light," said Wayne. "Thank God for the checklist bringing the shades was an essential," said Matt. "We wouldn't be able to see a foot in front of us with this amazing light," said Mark. "Should we approach it?" asked Sam. "It might bring us into another dimension," said Sam. "Sam you have been watching too much of the twilight zone with your brother. Don't say that I didn't warn you guys,"

"Let's get this over with and stop milking it," said Matt. They rowed into the light expecting something to happen. "I told you guys it is just the moonlight and it is nothing to be afraid of," said Wayne. "When God said let there be light, he wasn't kidding," said Matt. "That odor is putrid," said

Sam. "What is it?" said Sam. "It is probably the swamp. It gives off a tremendous smell," grinned Wayne. "No, you didn't do it to us again," said Mark. "I couldn't help it. I ate hot dogs and beans and too much candy," said Wayne. "It smells so bad back here I can't see," said Matt.

"Let's go a little further, perhaps there is something around the corner," said Wayne. "That is what I'm afraid of," said Sam. "Is this really worth it?" asked Mark. "I think we have a party pooper in the boat," said Matt. "We can leave you off at the next lily pad and pick you up on the way back," said Wayne.

"Oh, you guys are so generous and thoughtful and that is the reason I love you. I'll stay in the boat and watch the scenery," said Mark. "How about you Sam?" asked Matt. "Like Wayne said I'm good, but let's not run into any mutant frogs around the corner," said Sam.

Wayne put out his arm as a directional. They slowly turned right moving deeper into the swamp as it seemed to engulf the boat. "Let's admit that we are lost and that the treasure probably doesn't even exist," said Sam. "Let's not give up hope, Daniel son," laughed Matt. "You want to see karate, I'm a tenth-degree black belt. I'll show you my Kung Fu grip," said Sam. "Girls, girls enough back there. We have already come this far and we are not turning back," said Wayne.

"I see a sign posted ahead. I think it says that the treasure is this way," laughed Mark. "I think the swamp has got to him and he is seeing mirages," laughed Matt. "If I thought it would have been this long of a trip, I would have brought my pillow and baby blanket," said Sam.

All of a sudden, the boat began to shake. "Hey guys, don't rock the boat back there I'm trying to concentrate," said Wayne. "I told you guys it is probably one of those mutant frogs that want to capsize the boat," said Sam. "Get a hold of yourselves and row us out of here," said Wayne. "We are rowing, but we are not going anywhere," said Mark.

They became startled when the rod which was next to Wayne began to shimmer. They heard a loud thunder and noticed a bright light emanating from the antique rusty rod. The light was so powerful. It penetrated through several trees leaving a flaming arrow on each one. The boat slowly stopped and there was a silence for a few minutes. The only noises one could hear were the frogs, crickets and the birds.

They were stunned. "Hit me if I'm dreaming," said Matt. "Ok if you say so," said Mark. He lifted up his oar and hit Matt slightly on the side of the head. "Ouch dude! I'm awake that will leave a mark on me in the morning," said Matt. "Hold on guys, I left some seaweed hanging from your ear," said Mark.

Wayne glanced at his friends and noticed that Sam had passed out. "Someone help Sam and wake him up," said Wayne. Mark threw some water on Sam's face. Sam awakened and asked "What happened guys?" " know that we were in the right place at the right time. We have found our next clue," said Wayne.

They screamed in unison celebrating the moment. Their voices sent the birds into flight from their nests. "Guys, can you believe that as teenagers we are finding the treasure that no one thought existed?" asked Wayne. They looked at the flaming arrows as far as the eye could see until they faded into murkiness.

They switched places. Mark sat in the front while Wayne and Matt rowed and Sam sat in the back. "It almost looks like an illuminated runway," said Sam. Wayne and Matt continued rowing following the flaming arrows. As they passed the arrows one by one it would extinguish itself. "Well there goes our bread trail," said Matt. The arrows seem to veer off to the left up ahead," said Mark. "We are on it guys, left it is," said Wayne.

The boys were well into their journey. They were like little kids again in a candy store anxiously awaiting a new flavor to arrive. This time they were not waiting. They used their God given will. They were finding out that they were not kids anymore. With age came responsibility and maturity as they became adults.

"1 think we are running out of arrows. I only see three more," said Mark. They passed the last arrow as it finally extinguished itself. "Well back to square one guys," said Sam. "Let's not stop now. Keep rowing maybe we will encounter something up ahead," said Mark. "That is what I'm afraid of," said Sam.

They rowed very slowly searching for any signs of their next clue. "I can see a fork up ahead about one hundred yards," said Mark. "Should we take a right or a left?" asked Matt. "We have been having pretty good luck with the left," said Wayne. "1 think our luck just ran out because our boat is taking in water!" yelled Sam. The water rose above their feet. "Sam, take that bucket and start bailing us out. Matt and I will continue rowing as quickly as we can to that marsh in front of us," said Wayne. "I'm bailing as fast as I can guys, but the water seems to keep rising," yelled Sam. "1 think we will all have to make a swim for it," yelled Mark. "We will make it guys you must have faith," yelled Wayne. Wayne and Matt were sweating profusely rowing with all of their strength. "1 think that we are going to make it another twenty feet," said Wayne.

"Mark, you need to take the bucket, my arm has just given out," said Sam. Sam tossed the bucket to Mark and he started bailing out the water. "We are almost there guys. It is just a few more feet," said Wayne. Then the boat hit the marsh so hard the boys were tossed out of the boat landing in the marsh.

"Land ahoy! We made it! I don't believe it, but we made it," yelled Sam. They stood there exhausted for several minutes. "This marsh feels more like solid land," said Wayne. "1 think that you are right," said Mark. "Guys, let's pull the boat up on the land and fix the hole in it," said Matt.

They pulled the boat up on the land and began looking for the hole. "We have been looking for twenty minutes and neither one of us can find a hole," said Mark. "The water came into the boat and when we pulled it up on the land the water was gone; however, we have not found the hole," said Wayne. "It doesn't make any sense at all. I mean all of our feet are wet along with our sneakers. We couldn't have imagined it," said Matt. "Will someone explain why there isn't a hole in our boat?" asked Matt.

'"Guys, please hear me out. We have seen some strange things on our journey to locate the treasure. Once we passed that last arrow, we didn't have any sense of direction and that is when we began to take in water," said Wayne. "What if by taking in water we were driven here by some kind of powerful force?" asked Wayne. "Now who is watching too much of the twilight zone?" asked Sam. "Maybe so, but how do you explain it?" asked Wayne. "Ok let's just way that you are right. I don't see a clue or the treasure," said Mark. "It is probably out in the distance among the trees, so let's get our backpacks and start searching," said Wayne.

CHAPTER THIRTY-FOUR

WHERE DO WE GO FROM HERE?

"l think that someone should stay behind with the boat," said Sam. 'Suit yourself, but this is about the time the bats come out and search for blood," said Wayne. "Yeah, and they have strength in numbers, but you won't have a chance," said Matt. "We are wasting time. Leave him with the boat if that is what he wants," said Mark.

They left Sam and the boat behind until the darkness engulfed the three souls. "l'm safer staying behind with the boat. I'll just sit here in the boat and wait until they come back. He sat there in silence since he was alone. It was so still that all he could hear were the wild life in the swamp and their noises became more amplified. Sam couldn't take it any longer. "Guys, wait up for me!" said Sam. "You were right about the strength in numbers," said Sam. Sam caught up with the boys. "Look guys here is our fearless leader," said Wayne.

"l think that you should take the rod out of the backpack," said Mark. Wayne took it out and held it with a firm grip in his right hand. "If we ever find the treasure what are you guys going to do with your share?" asked Wayne. "I've thought about it and we all know that the first ten percent is given to God because he comes first and I will probably give the rest to my parents, and I will purchase the latest video games, music, college and a future home," said Mark.

"l think that we all agree that God comes first and give the rest to our parents to retire. Also, I would like to take a trip around the world and visit different countries and of course, a lifetime supply of Apple Jacks," said Wayne. "I would just want us to be friends for life and have many adventures in the future," said Sam.

With the rest of the money Sam you could purchase pumpkin seeds," laughed Matt. "What about you dude?" asked Wayne. "I think that I'll start making BMX bikes more rugged and durable so it can take jumps without being twisted like a pretzel upon impact," said Matt. "Now that we all know each other's dreams; this calls for a celebration. Break out the soda pop and tons of candy," said Wayne. "Raise your sodas please, here is to the future," said Wayne. They put their sodas together and took a sip. "Ah, that truly is the right stuff," said Mark.

"Hold up guys, we came to a dead end," said Matt. They looked straight ahead facing the swamp. "Over here, I think I have found our next clue," said Mark. "What is it?" asked Sam. "Look there are approximately a dozen rocks with some sort of painted symbols crossing over to that land mass," said Mark. "That is cool guys. The moonlight illuminates the symbols making them more visible," said Wayne. "What do the symbols mean?" asked Sam. "I don't know. What do I look like the information booth?" asked Wayne. "I was just asking you. You don't have to get bent out of shape," said Sam. "Relax, I was just playing with you, but I really don't know what they mean," said Wayne.

"To me, the symbols look a lot older than four to five hundred years. I think they are one trillion years old," said Matt. "Whatever they mean this is where I think we should cross," said Wayne. "Oh no! I'm not crossing on those slippery rocks. On another occasion, I saw people stepping on what looked like a rock, but it was a man-eating crocodile," said Sam. "Don't worry crocodiles don't live in New England. It is all about taking your time and using your balancing skills. We will all make it across safely," said Wayne.

Wayne started out on the rocks. One by one, he made his way closer to the other side. Mark followed behind and then Matt. Sam hesitated for one moment, but he took a chance on the rocks. They did find the rocks challenging with all of the slime. It almost made it impossible to cross. Even with Wayne's balancing skills, he found himself with one foot slipping into the swamp.

Sam found himself doing the splits on one of the rocks. Mark almost fell head first into the swamp, but fortunately, he regained his balance.

Matt slipped on one rock finding himself halfway in the swamp with his arms wrapped around the rock.

Wayne jumped from the last rock to solid ground. Mark and Matt made it as well. They looked back as Sam who was a little more than halfway. "Sam, come on you can do it!" yelled Mark. "You only have three more to go," said Matt. Sam planted his feet firmly on the next one. "Hey guys, those rocks have symbols on each one, right?" asked Sam. "Yeah, so what is the problem?" asked Wayne. "That's what I was afraid of because this one doesn't," said Sam. Sam began to panic and with pure adrenaline hurdled the last two in the air until he hit the ground. "I made it, I really made it! I could have been food for the crocodiles. That was a close one," said Sam. "It was only a snapping turtle, chill," said Matt.

Mark helped Sam up from the ground. "Sam, are you alright?" asked Wayne. "Let's see what is around the next corner waiting for us," said Wayne. "Just think if we ever find the treasure, we will have to return using the same routes; otherwise, we will venture to the other side," said Matt. "I think that there is much more to come. Let's see what this place has in store for us," said Matt.

CHAPTER THIRTY-FIVE

WATCHFUL EYES

"Now be careful guys, a place like this could have quicksand," said Wayne. "Thanks for the warning," said Sam. "I don't know where we are, but I'm pretty sure this is not the swamp. It looks like we are back in Gardner somewhere, but I can't place it," said Mark. "Are we lost, or did we just go completely around in a circle?" asked Wayne. "Speaking of circles, ever since we crossed over those rocks and stepped foot on this land, I've had a strange feeling that someone is watching us," said Matt.

"If I have to break out my ninja skills to protect my friends, I will," said Wayne. Wayne immediately went into his ninja stance. "See that guys, they always run to the hills with that one," said Wayne. "I put on my athletic socks this morning. I probably can run faster than they can," said Mark. "Now that we have our protective devices out of our system, which way shall we go?" asked Sam. "Why don't we take a right for a change?" asked Wayne.

They followed the amazing landscape to the right. "I've never seen such enormous trees and even the plant life is so vibrant," said Mark. "What are you a florist?" asked Matt. "No, I just love nature and all of God's beauty," said Mark. "Is there anything wrong with that?" asked Mark. "I guess not, since you put it that way," said Matt.

Wayne looked up and saw the trees covering them like a blanket and very little moonlight. suppose we can take our shades off for now because we can hardly see in front of us," said Wayne. They removed their shades except for Matt. "Are you taking your shades off?" asked

Sam. "Sam I am cool, calm and collected. I don't have any need to remove my shades," said Matt.

Suddenly, they heard a loud screeching noise which seemed to be in close proximity to where they were located. A rod of light that was in Wayne's hand disappeared into the night. "Hey guys, did you see what just happened?" asked Wayne. "It happened so fast and whatever came out of the sky was quicker than a bolt of lightning," said Mark. "It took our lifesaver too. It had to be very powerful to rip it out of my hands," said Wayne. "Did anyone see what it was?" asked Sam. "With these shades, I can't see anything," said Matt. "I hope we didn't need that rod anymore," said Wayne.

"Stop! Be quiet! I hear something," said Mark. "It sounds like rushing water," said Sam. Wayne ran ahead and almost went over the ravine. Wayne grabbed his chest because his heart was beating too fast. He fell to the ground and the guys caught up to him. "I thought that you were certainly going over the falls," said Sam. "Yeah, those rapids down there would have carried your body downstream never to be found," said Mark.

"Well, aren't we a cheerful group! I saw it coming all along. I had everything under control," said Wayne. "Why did you grab your chest?" asked Matt. "I was running at great speed when you saw me. Anyway, I wanted to see how close I could come to the edge without going over," said Wayne. "Help me guys, I think I scraped my hands from sliding," said Wayne. "You scraped more than that," said Mark. He pointed to Wayne's head.

They looked over the edge. "That is a long way down and it reminds me of the Grand Canyon," said Matt. "You can't make a cannonball off this without getting a few bumps and bruises," said Sam. "I just found our escape plan over the ravine," said Wayne. He pointed to a rope bridge approximately one hundred feet long. They went over to check it out.

"Oh no guys. We have to draw the line somewhere. Who knows if the bridge is deteriorated?" asked Sam. "I think Sam finally hit the nail on the head. We have come this far finding all of the clues and coins which led us here. We know that the treasure is real. So, let's go home. I mean it has been a great journey with all of us, but it is not worth risking our lives," said Mark. "Guys you know that I'm not a quitter and I know that you are not quitters either. I mean you guys would never have come this far if you were," said Wayne.

"I've been through blood, sweat and tears on this journey," said Wayne. "Did I say tears?" asked Wayne. "Well, maybe not tears, but we have come too far to turn back now. I'm not going to test God with my life, but I'm believing in God to take us through this experience unscathed," said Wayne. "You can turn back now, but I want to see what is on the other side of this bridge," said Wayne. "I'm not leaving my brother guys," said Matt. "Neither are we," said Mark and Sam.

"If all of us are going to cross the bridge, then I will go first and when I'm halfway then the next person should cross," said Wayne. "Look guys across the bridge on that post," said Sam. They saw an eagle in gold color. "The eagle has our rod of light in its claws," said Wayne. "I guess we found our culprit who has been watching over us," said Matt.

Wayne began to cross the old bridge. The boards made a slight cracking noise with each step. Wayne held the ropes on both sides to balance himself on the swaying bridge. "That is one brave guy to go out there without any fear," said Sam. "Leave your fear behind because we are going next," said Matt.

Once Wayne made it to the halfway point, Mark began to cross. "You can go next Sam. I'll have your back," said Matt. "You might want to take those shades off to see what you are doing," said Sam. "Guy when you are cool, you are cool," said Matt. The golden eagle flew away leaving the rod behind. "Ok Sam, it is your turn to go," said Matt. Sam tested the boards before crossing. '{Go ahead guy, I'm right behind you," said Matt. Sam made his way out on the bridge. "Whatever you do Sam, don't look down," said Matt. "Don't look down and have no fear," Sam spoke to himself.

"Be careful guys, some of the boards might break under your weight," said Wayne. "Now, he tells us not to have fear," said Sam. Matt was patiently waiting for his turn to cross. He was hoping that all of them would make it across without a scratch. Mark was almost there when his right leg went through one of the boards. His heart skipped a beat, but he remained focused. He pulled himself up by using the ropes. 'I l guess we have proven that theory," said Mark. "Well there goes one without a scratch," said Matt.

Mark made it across and Matt ventured out onto the bridge. Sam checked the boards before he put his weight on them. Sam was moving too slow and Matt was moving too fast. "Guys keep your distance and you don't want to put a strain on the ropes," said Wayne. "Guy, look the ropes are beginning to unravel," said Mark. "Run as fast as you can the ropes are about to snap," said Wayne. Sam and Matt didn't hesitate running not unlike the horses in the Kentucky Derby. "Run and don't look back," yelled Mark.

Steve was close to the edge, but Matt was still far behind. They heard what sounded like firecrackers and the ropes snapped causing the bridge to literally descend towards the ravine. Sam made a jump towards the edge and matt seized the rope. Sam clung onto the edge with his fingertips, but Wayne and Mark were quick enough to pull him to safety before he plummeted to his death.

"Oh my God, Matt, did anyone see him grab the rope?" asked Wayne. "l can't see him over the edge because there are too many jagged rocks in the way," said Mark. "Hello down there, can you hear me?" asked Wayne. There wasn't an answer. "It is my fault! I should have listened to you guys and turned around to return home. I thought the bridge was safe. They don't construct them like they used to," said Wayne.

"I think that pertains to cars," said Sam. "Can't I mourn without any criticism?" asked Wayne.

Suddenly, they heard a faint voice. "Hello up there!" said Matt. "Did everyone leave me?" asked Matt. "He's alive guys! He's alive! Grab that rope and we will pull him up slowly," said Wayne. "Hang on down there we will slowly pull you up," yelled Wayne. "What else can I do?" asked Matt. All of the boys pulled on the rope a few feet at a time. "It is taking them a long time to pull me up at this rate, I'll be late for my own wedding," said Matt.

"l see him guys. We have you Matt," said Wayne. They pulled on the rope once more. Matt remained on the ground looking up at the full moon and the stars. "l guess you will have to count your lucky stars tonight," said Sam. "I yelled to you, but didn't hear an answer. We thought you were gone," said Wayne. "Well, I hit solid rock which doesn't move for you and it knocked the wind out of me for a few minutes. I will have bruised ribs for one week," said Matt.

Sam looked back with a sigh. "How are we getting back home now genius?" asked Sam. "We will just have to build a large catapult and test it with you first Sam," said Wayne. "You can't be serious," said Sam. "I'm very serious. I still have my sister's hammer. I can build anything," said Wayne. "Maybe there is another way out around here," said Matt. "Put that on the agenda next to treasure," said Wayne.

CHAPTER THIRTY-SIX

UTOPIA

"l saw the eagle when it took off and went down the path straight ahead of us," said Wayne. "Grab that rod which it left behind just in case we need it again," said Mark. "I think after all we have experience, we are worthy of the treasure," said Sam. "l don't see the eagle anywhere," said Mark. "We will keep going because I'm certain that we will see it later," said Wayne. "Maybe he has the answer to all of the questions which brought us here," said Matt. "We might find out sooner than we think because I can hear him ahead," said Wayne.

They turned the corner and saw the bird perched up on one side of the tree limbs. The bird took flight over a hill approximately one hundred yards ahead of their trail. '"He must be the guide on this tour," said Sam. "Guys, do my legs look massive to you?" asked Matt. "Why do you ask a question like that at a time like this?" asked Mark. "Because of the hiking my legs feel massive," said Matt. "Ok guy, your legs look massive now let's go," said Sam. "That's what I thought they are really massive," said Matt. "We might want to move away from Matt because he has a monumental ego," said Wayne.

"Be careful guys, that eagle might be leading us into a trap. There might be a cliff over that hill so keep an eye out for anything suspicious," said Mark. "Are you coming Arnold?" laughed Sam. "I need a tan to get more definition in my legs," said Matt. "You will need someone with large legs to carry the gold," said Matt.

"We should pull our weight," said Matt. "Let's see what lies ahead over that hill," said Wayne. "Lead on Sherlock, we are right behind you," said Mark. Looking up at the hill from the bottom it looks more like a mountain," said Sam. "When you grow taller with some platform shoes it will look like a hill," laughed Matt. "Platform shoes you don't say, I'll look into that," said Sam. "I don't see an easy way up," said Wayne. "That human catapult would have come in handy right now," said Wayne.

Sam wanted to know why he had to be the first to take on the challenge. "Because you are the type of man that can handle any challenge and dominate from the past to the future," said Wayne. Sam felt a bolt of lightning pass through him and he stood taller. His face illuminated not unlike the stars in the sky and his arms extended out from his torso with his head held high.

A light opened up in the night and shined on Sam. "Look at Sam! He looks different, like could take on the world. You look like a conqueror. "Let's conquer the hill like it didn't exist," said Sam. Whenever we ascend the hill there had better be a treasure on it," said Wayne. "Mark it might be better if we zig zag from left to right that way, so that we won't sprain our ankles or break our legs on the rocky terrain," said Wayne. "I'll go first this time," said Sam. Pushing Mark, Matt and Wayne aside, he demonstrated how to climb the mountain that is standing in their way.

Sam led the way climbing the hill without hesitation. "I think if we have another obstacle in our way, we will use dynamite to blow it up," said Mark. They followed Sam about halfway up the hill. "We are near the top and I hope that the eagle doesn't dive on us when we arrive there," said Sam.

"Careful guys, I almost twisted my ankle on the rock right there," said Sam. "I think that we should stop here by this large rock and refuel," said Wayne. "Good idea. I think that I will get a root beer and some of those bottle caps," said Mark. "Rock candy for me guys," said Wayne. "I think that I will have a few of those pixie sticks," said Matt.

"I'll have a Three Musketeers bar or should I say four?" asked Sam. "I have enough sugar in me now to go for a few more hours," said Wayne. They ascended to the top of the hill. They stood at thesummit speechless and in awe. Their eyes gazed down in the valley. "Someone slap me. I think that I'm having the best dream of my life," said Sam.

Matt went over and slapped Sam in the face. "Ouch! Guy not so hard," said Sam. As the pain subsided, Sam began to smile again.

CHAPTER THIRTY-SEVEN

THE OLD SETTLEMENT

Mark began jumping up and down. 'We found it, we really found it! The village of the first settlers. Imagine all of the history, this is just amazing!" said Mark. "Everything we had to endure to get here, it was definitely worth it," said Wayne.

They slowly descended the hill still attempting to absorb all of the adventure. "Look guys by the large fire pit. They probably never used it to cook their food," said Matt. The golden eagle was perched upon one of the rocks. "Never mind him guys. I still don't see any treasure," said Matt. "Maybe this is it and we are standing right in the middle of it," said Sam. "Let's check out some of the small cottages that are still standing," said Sam.

They separated and explored the seven cottages. Approximately one hour later, they met over by the fire pit. "Anyone come up with the treasure or any clues?" asked Wayne. "AII I saw was rotted furniture and old pots and pans, not much else," said Mark. "Same here guy," said Matt. They looked at Sam who was wearing old spectacles. "What did you find Professor Genius?" asked Wayne.

"Using my intellectual knowledge and my twenty-twenty vision, how would I articulate it for my students to understand?" asked Sam. "Oh yeah, I found nothing" said Sam. "How about you student one?" asked Sam. "Do you see me with gold sitting on my lap?" asked Wayne. "Excellent point, excellent point," said Sam.

"There's plenty of history here for those guys in Boston to get their hands on, but we expected to find the treasure. I thought deep in my heart that when we saw the village that we would find the treasure as well and then we could finally get a good night's sleep," said Mark. "Not even another clue," said Matt. "Even if there was another clue right in front of us, we wouldn't know it," said Sam.

"Who brought the instant coffee?" asked Wayne. "We could start a small fire in the pit and drink some coffee and contemplate on our next move. Sam you could gather some small sticks and Mark you could find a pot that we can put water into," said Wayne. "They are all filthy guy," said Mark. "Rinse it out with a little water. Besides, a little dirt never hurt anyone," said Mark. "Matt, did you get the newspaper?" asked Wayne. "Just kidding guy," said Wayne. "What are you going to do?" asked Mark. "l have the Bic. I'll flick the Bic to start the fire," said Wayne.

They sat around the fire with their cups of coffee. "Nothing like one half of a cup of sugar and the rest coffee with a drop of milk," said Wayne. "Best way to consume it. It is like having the best of both worlds," said Mark. "l guess we will have to face it guys. If there was a treasure, it has been gone a long time," said Matt.

"Because there are signs of the old settlers, so they never left, which means the treasure is still here. We just haven't looked hard enough," said Wayne. "We really can't give up now guys because we have come so far. Come on guys, help me look once more," said Wayne.

The guys sat drinking their coffee. "Let's face it, we have been swindled all along and we should just dust ourselves off and get out of here. We have great memories and not so great ones. We will hold on to the great ones. I'm sure we will have many more" said Mark. "Put your hands in and then we can celebrate our lives with an ice-cold glass of milk. Who is with me?" asked Mark. Matt and Sam put their hands in, but Wayne sat there in deep thought. "Well, we did find several clues. We laughed and cried and I won't mention any names, but look at the party and whistle. I

think that we can finally say we accomplished our goal and that is the friendship. I'm in guys, let's get out of here," said Wayne.

They tossed their cups into the fire pit. They looked back at the hill and turned around. "Maybe we can find a quicker way out this way. Do you think we should tell Mr. Stevens about this place?" asked Sam.

They looked at one another. "Nah! Let them keep looking," they said as they laughed.

"Wait a minute guys. I forgot my backpack and we forgot to put the fire out," said Wayne. They ran back towards the fire pit. "'Look guys, that eagle has my backpack," said Wayne. The eagle swooped down and dropped the backpack into the fire. "That's just great because my shades are in there with the rod of light. Hurry, grab a stick and get my bag out," said Wayne.

The earth began to shake, knocking them to the ground. "Earthquake!" yelled Sam. "In Gardner hey!" said Wayne. "The ground is cracking. I told you we would be engulfed into the abyss," said Matt.

The cottages began to collapse and the moonlight illuminated the area. They closed their eyes so as not to be blinded by the light. "We have to try to get out of here, but the light is too bright for us to see one foot in front of us," said Wayne. They heard a loud noise. "Was that you Wayne?" asked Mark. "It wasn't me this time," said Wayne.

The light was absorbed by the fire. They were able to see once again. It seemed as quickly as the light disappeared an indescribable one emitted out of the fire illuminated the hillside. The side of the hill began to disintegrate. "Run for your lives!" yelled Mark.

Sam ran behind a large tree. The rocks continued falling, but minutes later stopped. The entire hillside became debris. The shaking of the earth came to a screeching halt. Wayne quickly put out the fire with the water, but he couldn't save his backpack. "That's just great! My two- dollar shades are destroyed. I've had them for ten years, ever since our parents brought us to Hampton Beach. I bought them in a five and dime store. They were my lucky shades," said Wayne.

"Guys, do you really think that was an earthquake?" asked Matt. "I don't think there was ever an earthquake in Gardner," said Mark. "Well, explain all of the earth shaking and the extraordinary bright light?" asked Matt. "Perhaps, it was a meteor which fell in the near vicinity. I think that we should check it out. Maybe we will get a chance to see a real live extraterrestrial," said Mark.

"You are dreaming guy. The only time you will see them is in one of those science fiction movies," said Wayne. "It's over guys. We should split before anything else happens," said Matt. Wayne pointed up at the eagle perched on the rubble. "It's your fault, you dirty bird," said Wayne. "I think he is giving you the evil eye. I think he wants a piece of you," said Sam. "He's not only going to get a piece, but I will use my ninja skills that no one has ever seen before," said Wayne.

"Guys, I think we have this all wrong. The eagle has been following us probably since the beginning, but we never noticed until now. Maybe the treasure is here and he's trying to tell us something," said Matt. "If he is trying to tell us something, he really is going about it in the wrong way by destroying my backpack," said Wayne. "Yeah, but I think he knew the rod of light was in there and I think it created all of this destruction," said Matt. "Why destroy all of the history from which one can learn?" asked Mark.

"Guy where did the eagle go?" asked Matt. "I think he hid behind the rubble," said Sam. "Let's check it out because he is starting to make me wonder where we should go from here," said Wayne.

They began to climb up the hill which had become debris. "I can't wait for the time when we don't have to climb anything. I need to give my ankles a rest," said Mark. They finally reached the top of the debris. "Look at all of the barrels which are enclosed within the hillside. They are stacked two, three even four feet high," said Sam. "There has to be seventy-five to one hundred barrels here," said Mark. "What do you think is inside of them?" asked Matt. "Could it be another clue?" asked Sam. "Let's break one open and find out," said Wayne.

They climbed down to the barrels. "We will break the top one with a sharp rock," said Mark. Matt picked up a rock and hit the top of the barrel. "What are you giving it a love tap?" asked Mark. "Hit it hard," said Mark. Matt raised the rock above his head coming down will all of his might splitting the wood. "I can't wait to see what is inside of it," said Sam. Mark and Matt lifted up the wood, tearing it away from the barrel. "What is in it guys?" asked Sam. Matt retrieved several scrolls. "There is a lot of history contained in these barrels," said Matt. They looked disappointed since they were hoping to find the treasure. "Well, I guess the historians from Boston will be in all of their glory when we show them what we have discovered," said Mark.

"I'm on top of the world!" yelled Wayne as he stood on top of the barrels. "Yeah, we noticed you had better be careful up there before you fall," said Matt. "Careful is my middle name," said Wayne. "I thought it was conqueror?" asked Sam. "That is another one. I have tons of middle names," said Wayne.

Wayne began to lose his balance on the barrel. The barrel quickly kicked out from under his feet.

The barrel fell to the rocks below splitting open and Wayne fell on top. "Guys, look!" yelled Matt. Wayne reached below him with his hands pulling up hundreds of gold coins.

"Guys, I can't believe we finally found the lost treasure!" yelled Mark. "I never thought that when I fell from a barrel that gold coins would cushion my fall, but I love it!" said Wayne. Wayne poured the gold coins over his head. They seized the gold coins and let them slip through their hands making a game of it. "What a great feeling!" said Sam. "Most of these barrels must have been filled with gold coins," said Matt.

They climbed back on top of the debris and sat down. "Some journey guys and it came with a joyful ending," said Wayne. They collectively made a sigh of relief. I wonder what happened to the golden eagle?" asked Sam. "There he is flying into the beautiful sunrise," said Mark. "Sunrise!" yelled Wayne and Matt. "Right about now, our parents are finding out that we weren't home all night," said Wayne. "Relax guys, after they find out that we found the treasure, they will forget all about last night," said Mark. "Let's find our way out of here and get a hold of the historians from Boston," said Wayne. "That should be really easy," said Matt.

CHAPTER THIRTY-EIGHT

CHURCH ON TIME

"Well guys, our parents were pretty cool after we told them the entire story. Mr. Stevens, our friend from Boston, agreed to give a large portion to Christians in our name and to the museum. He further stated that we could go to the museum whenever we wanted to see it on display. The gold coins are worth trillions of dollars. They handed our parents a check. I always told you that Mr. Stevens and company were cool dudes," said Wayne.

"It always seems like a long walk to the church," said Sam. Wayne opened the door to the church a crack. He poked his head inside to look for a moment. "What are you doing?" asked Mark. "I said I was only going to look inside," said Wayne. Mark pushed Wayne through the door and they attended the service.

They exited the church. "Guys, that was truly amazing! I know I'm going to love God and his son Lord Jesus Christ and the Holy Spirit," said Wayne. They formed a circle and held each other's hands. They said a prayer thanking God for his love and peace in the world. Amen.

CHAPTER THIRTY-NINE

THE CHALLENGE

"This is it guys! We agreed on pulling out our homemade Go Karts from last year instead of our BMX's. The challenge is that we start at the top of the hill and when I say go, we shoot down the hill. It is probably two hundred yards. Then we shoot off the cliff below and whoever makes it the furthest in the S. Bents lumberyard wins," said Wayne. "What did you make you Go Kart out of, toothpicks?" said Matt. "Talk is cheap. I want to see you fly off that cliff and come in last. My toothpicks will blow your doors off," said Sam. They lined their Go Karts up evenly. "Are you ready? Get set! Go!" yelled Wayne.

Wayne pulled out ahead then Sam's toothpick mobile began passing Wayne. Matt came on strong and then Mark. A few toothpicks flew off Sam's Go Kart. "Stay together baby we have got this," said Sam. "Warped speed!" yelled Wayne. Mark's back tire began to shake. "Hang in there, we are almost there," said Wayne. Mark's back tire finally fell off creating sparks off the pavement. He didn't lose much speed.

"Here we go, hold on tight guys. Now is the time to stop if you want to chicken out!" said Wayne. "Bring it on!" they yelled in unison. They shot off the cliff getting tons of air. Dudes!